Tessa met his eyes.

In Drake's eyes was not only intelligence but gentleness and need. She wasn't sure what he needed, but it was there in his eyes. Without another word, she held out her pet parrot, which transferred itself onto his shoulder. She silently vowed at that moment to stop staring at this man.

His voice interrupted her thoughts. "Wow."

Her gaze went to him. His eyes sparkled with pleasure and his teeth showed when he smiled. Grinning up at her, he winked. "Pirate."

She returned his grin, then turned to go back up the ramp. Even with her back to Drake, the spell over her emotions was still in full force. She wondered if there was such a thing as meeting someone that you just knew was going to play an important part in your life—like God saying, "Look here, don't miss this. He's important to you."

If so, then Tessa was certain that was what had just happened to her.

Books by Cheryl Wolverton

Love Inspired

A Matter of Trust #11
A Father's Love #20
This Side of Paradise #38
The Best Christmas Ever #47
A Mother's Love #63
For Love of Zach #76
For Love of Hawk #87
For Love of Mitch #105
Healing Hearts #118

*Hill Creek, Texas

CHERYL WOLVERTON

grew up in a military town, though her father was no longer in the service when she was born. She attended Tomlinson Junior High School and Lawton High School, and was attending Cameron when she met her husband, Steve. After a whirlwind courtship of two weeks they became engaged. Four months later they were married, and that was over seventeen years ago.

Cheryl and Steve have two wonderful children, Christina, sixteen, and Jeremiah, thirteen. Cheryl loves having two teenagers in the house.

As for books, Cheryl has written nine novels for the Steeple Hill Love Inspired line and is currently working on new novels. You can contact Cheryl at P.O. Box 207, Slaughter, LA 70777. She loves to hear from readers.

Healing Hearts
Cheryl Wolverton

Published by Steeple Hill Books™

STEEPLE HILL BOOKS

Steeple
Hill™

ISBN 0-373-87124-4

HEALING HEARTS

Copyright © 2000 by Cheryl Wolverton

Visit us at www.steeplehill.com

Printed in U.S.A.

...we do not lose heart. Though outwardly we are wasting away, yet inwardly we are being renewed day by day. For our light and momentary troubles are achieving for us an eternal glory that far outweighs them all. So we fix our eyes not on what is seen, but on what is unseen. For what is seen is temporary, but what is unseen is eternal.

—II *Corinthians* 4:16-18

In the good times, in the bad times, in all times give thanks—to paraphrase a Bible verse. And that's what I want to do here—give thanks to my family for their love and their long-suffering patience. A writer who works at home could not succeed if their family did not support him or her. Thank you, dear ones, with the love in my heart.

Pam Schlutt, who has taken over my mailing lists, etc.... Pam, you are such a lifesaver. I would not have finished this book if you hadn't assisted me. Thank you, dear one.

And finally, to my Heavenly Father. Through the ups and downs, triumphs, disappointments, my Father is always there, my best friend, my confidant, my Father who laughs with me, holds me when I cry, but especially who died for me. Without Your love, Father, I would not know love. Thank You.

Chapter One

❧

"Tessa? Tessa?"

Tessa Stanridge heard her name and turned on her knees to locate her visitor. The soft ground, still slightly damp in the early morning hours, gave her easy access to pivot. She'd been watching her turtle build a nest for her soon-to-be eggs in her little fenced-in area. She loved to spend mornings outside. And her friend knew that well. That was obviously why she'd come to the backyard. "Back here, Dr. McCade," Tessa said.

She had taken quite nicely to the offbeat woman—a woman who reminded Tessa of

herself in some ways. Except that she wasn't
a doctor like Susan "Freckles" McCade, nor
was she married. She was simply a school-
teacher working to eke out a living in the
town of Hill Creek, Texas. A peaceful town,
quiet, a place to heal and recover.

Freckles McCade came around the corner,
hands curled in the pockets of her sweater
which she held against her body to fight off
the chill of the windy, late springlike weather
they were experiencing. Her red curls
bounced and her freckles—where she'd gotten her nickname from—stood out against her
pale skin. A huge grin spread across her face
when she spotted Tessa. "I'm so glad I found
you. I just might have some information for
you about a summer job."

That was Freckles. She always spoke what
was on her mind. Tessa smiled. "Good morning to you too, Susan." After pushing herself
up from the ground, Tessa stood and brushed
off her hands. Her turtle would be all right
for now. She'd check on her again later.
"Come in and have some tea."

Freckles chuckled, her cheeks turning pink. "Don't mind if I do."

Tessa started toward the back door. "Careful of your step," she warned. "We don't want you falling in your condition."

Freckles sighed dramatically. "I'm only a few weeks pregnant, Tessa. And stop referring to my pregnancy," she chided with a chuckle. "If you keep treating me differently, everyone is going to figure it out."

Tessa hurried up the wooden steps and pulled open the creaking door. She shoved it back, giving Freckles time to catch it as she entered the kitchen. Crossing the dark wooden floor she paused to rinse her hands at the old-fashioned porcelain sink.

Sam the parrot waddled over, his toenails clicking, his green and red feathers flapping as he perched himself upon the nozzle of running water. Moving the parrot to the side, Tessa paused to give him fresh water and peel a banana for him. After cutting it up, she slipped it into the holder on the large wooden table that was set up with perches and ropes and all kinds of paraphernalia just for Sam.

She then put on water to boil. "I'm not treating you differently," Tessa said lightly to Freckles.

Seeing Freckles attempting to warn off a rabbit that was insistent on nibbling at her toes where she sat, she chuckled. Going over, she seated herself at the rickety wooden table and nudged the rabbit's chew toy toward it. The rabbit promptly gave up Freckles's toes and happily went to work on his toy. "I treat all women in your condition the same."

Freckles sighed loudly. "Okay, Tessa. You win."

Tessa breathed a sigh of relief. Everyone knew how clumsy Freckles could be. The only one who would be surprised that Freckles was pregnant would be Freckles herself when she told everyone. It was obvious that Freckles carried a child. The woman glowed and her hand kept going to her abdomen. Her husband, Julian, walked around like the baby had already been born, pride shining off his face and his gaze constantly on his wife. And he was so careful with her it wasn't even laughable. If he could get away with packing her away in a padded room for her entire pregnancy, Tessa wouldn't doubt that Julian would do it.

Envy touched Tessa's heart. How she wanted children. How she wanted to care for someone, to nurture, to love. But she never would have a tiny one to hold.

Freckles touched a letter lying on her table. "Another one from Stan?"

Tessa glanced down at the letter. "Yeah. He has sent me a card weekly since Christmas."

"And you're just friends?" Freckles asked, amused.

The sound of the whistle from the teapot turned Tessa's attention to the stove. Tessa rose and crossed back to finish the tea. The echoing sound of her feet on the wooden floor made the room seem hollow and lonely. But that was how things were. She thought about Stan, how much he reminded her of someone else she'd known from her past. Just not really her type. "Yeah, just friends," she murmured to Freckles.

"Is he still threatening to come out here one day and sweep you off on a date?"

Pouring two cups of tea, she listened as Freckles paused to talk to the horned toad in a cage near the kitchen table.

While Tessa added sugar to the tea, the parrot, Sam, came to examine what she was doing before returning to his perch. "He tells me that every three or four weeks."

"He just doesn't let go, does he?" Freckles asked, then chuckled.

Carrying the two cups, Tessa went to the table and seated herself, handing a cup to Freckles. "Evidently not. But Freckles, no ideas of romanticism, please. He seems like a nice person but I'm just not interested in dating anyone. Now, how can I help you?" Freckles thought everyone should be married since she'd married. She was a matchmaker. Tessa didn't have the courage to tell Freckles she had been engaged to someone like Stan a long time ago, before the earthquake, before the accident... She was still healing emotionally from that.

Freckles took a slow sip of tea. "This

herbal blend is wonderful,'' she said. Closing her eyes, she smiled and inhaled the scent before taking another sip. Finally, she set her cup aside and met Tessa's gaze.

"I like my herbal teas,'' Tessa murmured dryly, knowing the townsfolk couldn't understand her desire for herbal tea and the fact that she didn't eat meat. Except for Freckles. Freckles had never questioned her eating habits or drinking habits—or lack thereof. Freckles was a dear friend she could trust with almost anything.

"I like your herbal teas now—especially now! Now, about that job.''

Tessa listened. She had no choice. She was desperate for a job though no one except Freckles and maybe her past friends from California knew—those that still knew she was on this earth, that was. She hadn't told Leah about it, though. And Leah was one of her closest friends here in Hill Creek. Fellow teacher at the local elementary school, she and Leah both taught the children during the year and found other work during the summer. Usually they held tutoring jobs.

"Have you found anything major yet to help your situation?"

"I have one or two people that are interested in hiring me to work with their children."

Freckles shook her head. "They wouldn't bring in enough for you to survive. You are way in debt from moving out here. You need cash and you need it fast to save this house. And I think I've found the answer."

Tessa perked up. Money to save the house? Just this morning, watching her turtles out back, Tessa was sure that by August she would be moving back to California where she could find a better-paying job. Old friends had offered several times to find her a job back in California if she ever came back. But God had led her here for a reason and she really didn't want to go back. For several reasons, including there were too many earthquakes, too many people and too many dark memories. She was happy here—except for the massive medical bills she had. It had gotten to the point that if she didn't get more money soon, she was going to lose everything. She wouldn't allow that, which meant moving back to where she knew there was a job waiting for her—a well-paying job.

Anything would be better right now than considering that. "Go on, Freckles, I'm listening."

Freckles grinned at Tessa. Then she sobered. "There is a man that needs tutoring. It's a rather private thing. His family doesn't want the town to know about his reading problem."

Tessa nodded. She well understood male pride and illiteracy. "What made him come to you?" she asked, curious.

The wind ruffled the bright yellow curtains, bringing in the morning smell of dew and lilacs. The parrot squawked and moved closer to the window, bobbing at the curtains. Absently, Tessa snapped her fingers and motioned for Sam to settle back on his perch.

Missy, her cat, wandered in and wove in and out of Tessa's legs before jumping into her lap and stretching. Tessa shifted, adjusting herself so Missy had the room she sought.

Stretching her paws, she finally settled into Tessa's lap.

"He didn't come to me, actually. He's a patient and he's currently in occupational therapy."

"Therapy?"

Tessa stroked Missy, tapping her nose when she eyed the parrot. The cat objected by flexing her claws in Tessa's leg then relaxed for petting.

"He's had symptoms that indicate he has had a minor cerebral hemorrhage."

"Oh dear," Tessa's brow furrowed. She knew all about strokes, from her mother. "How bad is it?"

"To put it simply, he's working on relearning to talk right now. He came into the hospital in critical condition and needed emergency surgery. I'm sure you heard the story of the accident." Freckles waved a hand indicating that this wasn't what she wanted to discuss. "Suffice it to say, during the surgery, the doctors were unable to repair everything. While they had him on the table working on him the cerebral hemorrhaging caused some damage. This has resulted in the trouble reading. Actually,'' Freckles said, picking up the spoon and absently stirring her tea, ''it's a miracle he lived at all. He had so many problems. He's doing marvelous considering what shape he was in when he was brought into the E.R.''

''Really? Thank God,'' Tessa said simply.

Freckles nodded. ''And God alone. Hope went out the window when he came through that emergency room door. We were working on him, but it was just so bad.'' Freckles leaned forward, her earnest look burning into Tessa. ''Someone wouldn't give up on him though. Someone stayed in the prayer closet because the man made it and he's healing at a phenomenal rate.''

Freckles paused to sip her tea. As silence fell, Tessa wondered if that was why she hadn't died when she'd been hurt. Had God simply been watching out for her? Had someone been praying, seeking God on her behalf? She was curious, which surprised her. It had been so long since she'd really shown interest in anything except her kids and animals.

"When he first started showing signs of improvement," Freckles continued now, "we thought it'd be months of therapy to see any progress, let alone to see him progress this far."

Freckles shook her head. "We were wrong, Tessa. He's proven that. It's hard to believe, but the patient is even talking already, though he still slurs his words a bit—especially if he gets stressed or upset."

Again Freckles leaned forward, her intense stare indicating how much this meant to her. "He's trying to read on his own, Tessa. He is doing more than any patient I've ever seen. But he needs help. You see—" Freckles reached down to pet the puppy that came trotting in to his water dish "—it's time for him to be dismissed but he lives too far outside of town for that. You know we don't have a rest home or a rehabilitation type place here in Hill Creek. There's no one near the hospital to take care of him. We want to keep him close by in case of developments...."

"I'm not really a nurse," Tessa began, stroking her cat.

"You don't have to be one," Freckles explained. Clasping her hands, she leaned forward eagerly. "You see, his brother has hired an occupational therapist. He needs a teacher."

"You said there was no one to take care of him though?" Tessa cut in, confused.

Freckles smiled. "There's no one to *care* for him. He needs someone to care while they teach him. Someone to be patient. Right now his younger brother is running the ranch and running scared if you ask me. Anyway, Liam loves Drake but just doesn't have enough time in the day to do everything. He needs someone who cares about what they do, Tessa, and that's you. His brother is really hoping to find someone who is compassionate to help him in the daytime and evenings. He'll have someone come out every morning to do Drake's therapy."

"The Slaters?" Shocked, Tessa stared. She had heard of the Slaters's place outside of town. They were big ranchers in these parts. They worked hard though rarely came into town, if rumors could be counted. It was a

long way out to their ranch though—almost
to the other county! "I can't go all the way
over there. It's nearly a two-hour drive."

"I realize that. So does Liam. He's offered
to pay you rent if you allow Drake to move
into your guestroom over on the side of the
house here."

"The guestroom!" Tessa gulped. "But—
in my house? Wait a minute…" Tessa tried
to make sense of what Freckles had just asked
her. True, this was an older house that had a
guestroom built on the outside of the house
for travelers that might need somewhere to
stay. She'd even used it for that once or
twice.

But…wow, this was certainly a lot to take
in. Just this morning she was certain she was
going to be saying goodbye to Hill Creek if
something didn't turn up soon. Then this
dropped in her lap. All of it. Like a ton of
bricks.

She had to hand it to Freckles. Tessa had
watched her bowl over other people before,
but this was the first time she'd shocked
Tessa.

"He's in a wheelchair," Freckles whispered, low.

"But...but...he can't move in here! I'm single." She could only imagine her neighbors and... *Wheelchair?* That gave her pause. The poor man was in a chair and needing assistance. He needed to be close to the hospital. A wheelchair.

"Even if you have a live-in chaperone?" Freckles said in her oh-so-tempting voice, her eyes dancing with mischief.

"Chaperone?" Tessa asked warily. She didn't like it when Freckles turned that mischievous look on her like that.

Freckles smiled. "Let me finish explaining."

Tessa felt the dark shock recede as Freckles's reassuring voice soothed her, but how could she convince her to take this job? "I'm not sure what you can add to what you've said already—"

"How about a thousand dollars a week and a live-in cook?" Freckles asked.

Tessa gaped as she listened to the details of just what the pay would be for and the extra allotments for the cook. She couldn't help but shake her head when Freckles finished the list of payments. That was more than she made as a teacher each month, that was for certain. "Why so much?" she asked, dumbfounded. That was all she asked because that was all she could get out. As a matter of fact, Tessa was suddenly sure she hadn't heard the woman in front of her correctly. Maybe she was dreaming and this was all simply a wishful, wonderful fantasy.

Freckles shoved Tessa's cup at her, bumping her hand. Tessa realized she was gripping the rim of the table—a very telling sign—and immediately released it.

"Drink this before you pass out."

Tessa didn't argue. She captured the cup and gulped it down. *A thousand dollars plus expenses...* Mentally she started tabulating the doctor's, radiologist's, and surgeon's bills that were awaiting her payments. "This is some kind of mistake," she whispered. "They don't pay that much for tutoring."

"No, but I've talked with Liam. I told you, Drake is a special case. He needs to get out of the hospital, but we, the team who has been working on his case, don't want him that far away from emergency treatment. Not yet, at least. Still, he's too well to stay in a bed at the hospital. Drake doesn't like the accommodations and is more than ready to leave. His brother's certain it's affecting him adversely to stay there when he is determined to progress.

"You live right here in town, near enough that if an emergency happens he could be to the hospital in five minutes. I happen to know you nursed your mother when she had a stroke and that, at one time, you had considered going into nursing."

"That's what I get for telling you all of my secrets," Tessa muttered. What Freckles said was true. But after all that had happened with her mother, then her own injuries...

Unable to sit still a moment longer, she stood and settled the cat in her chair. The cat protested.

The bird squawked at the cat and danced back and forth on his wooden perch. The puppy had finished drinking and now sniffed the floor, a sure indication he needed out. Tessa picked him up and took him out back to do his business. While she stood at the door she said, "What else?" Evidently Liam had thought of everything.

"Liam wanted to send a cook to make sure his brother got the right meals. The person would prepare all of the meals while here and either live in, if you wanted, or stay in someone else's house. However, Liam said that if the cook didn't live in then he would subtract that weekly allotment. But, I thought, since you might want a chaperone and all..."

Absently Tessa nodded. A thousand a week. A thousand dollars. She wouldn't have to go back to California. She could stay here in her house. She'd be in control of the situation. Control was very important to Tessa, especially in circumstances like this.

But the Slaters? She'd seen Liam—once. They were big men. Huge men. Living out here in Hill Creek, Texas, she had to wonder if all the men grew that big. Running her hands through her brown hair she twisted it into a knot, defying the morning wind to tear it loose again. Playing with her hair was a nervous habit of hers. She knew that. She tried not to do it, but the habit still surfaced—occasionally.

She heard Freckles stand, heard her move up behind her, making her way around the many creatures that occupied Tessa's house. Once by her side, Freckles stared out the screen door as well.

"It would be an answer to your financial problems, Tessa. God still does answer prayers, you know."

"Yes. It would help." That was easy to admit. "But does God answer a prayer by sending a man to live in my house? By sending me a cook? By paying me an outrageous sum just to play baby-sitter and tutor?"

Freckles smiled. "It looks like this time He does."

Tessa simply shook her head. "I just can't believe it."

"He's going to pay a month's salary in advance, Tessa. If you decide you can't handle it at the end of eight weeks, you'll get the full payment and Liam will find someone else."

"Why?"

"Liam is desperate to help his brother. When I told him you might be interested in the job he jumped at the chance, working to make the offer too good to refuse."

"It is that, I'll admit," Tessa murmured. She'd finally have the last of her medical bills paid off. There would be no more threatening letters from creditors, no more worries of losing everything, watching her credit die a certain death, losing everything because of the mountain of debt she'd been working to slowly pay off for three years now.

Tessa felt for the first time in a long time as if she was seeing a light at the end of the tunnel. "Is Liam willing to draw up a contract?"

Freckles grinned. Reaching in her pocket, she pulled out a folded document. "Already done."

Tessa laughed. She couldn't help it. "Awful arrogant of him, wouldn't you say?"

Freckles giggled. "No. He's just really hopeful. He wants his brother home. The sooner, the better."

Tessa took the contract and then hesitated as she stared at it.

"Come on, Tessa, what have you got to lose?" Freckles encouraged.

Tessa thought about the outside guestroom with its own private entrance, the lockable door between the outside and inside part of the kitchen. She thought about the cook moving in. She could put the woman in the extra room that she never used.

She thought about teaching someone to read and with third-graders knew she could do that easily. What did she have to lose?

Looking at Freckles she felt hope rise. Should she? Or should she not?

She might...

A wheelchair.

She could...

A chaperone.

Going over to a drawer in her kitchen, she opened it and pulled out a pen. With a quick read over the contract, she nodded and signed it. "You're right. I haven't a thing to lose."

Chapter Two

Except her mind. This was insane. "What is *that?*" Tessa demanded of the newest men coming in her door, hefting a huge box. Once she quickly dropped her letter in the mailbox, she stepped back out of the way.

"Freezer, ma'am." The man promptly bumped into the side of the door, grunting and shuffling his feet to keep from dropping the front end of his load.

"But why?" she cried, grabbing at the barking puppy who came into the kitchen and ran around their feet, nearly tripping an older round man.

"For the food," a younger man behind the two moving men informed her.

Sam squawked and flapped his wings. Heaven knew where her cat or any of her other animals were. Hiding most likely.

"Where'd you like it?"

"What?" she asked glancing back at the man with gray hair.

"The freezer, ma'am."

"Um, I—I…" Taking stock of her kitchen, she stroked the wiggling puppy. When Hubert the puppy wouldn't calm down, she went to the side room just off the kitchen and put him into the room before pulling the door closed. She heard the whining but did her best to block it from her mind.

Turning her attention back to the kitchen, she finally pointed to the parrot's perch. "We can put it there in front of the window and move Sam over here."

She started toward the parrot. "We'll get that ma'am," the older man broke in.

Sam protested their approach, hopping to the floor and waddling his way over to Tessa. She picked him up, and put him on her shoulder. She then quickly moved the stepping stool and smaller birdcage—for her toad— into the living room.

Why in the world was the man sending in a freezer? It had to be the Slaters. "I really don't need this," she told the men as they positioned the freezer.

"Orders, ma'am."

Tessa wondered if that was all the older man could say. She wanted to tell him her name was Tessa. She didn't. Instead, she opened her mouth to explain that her guest would only be here a short time when the phone rang.

"We'll put the food in the freezer, if that's okay with you, Miss Stanridge," the young delivery boy said, motioning to boxes of...something he'd brought with him.

Tessa didn't argue. She nodded and grabbed the ringing phone. "Hello?" After all, nothing could be worse than the disaster they were making of her kitchen.

"Tessa, guess who?"

Tessa paused at the deep voice on the other end of the phone line. Memories of her past, of what seemed to her like eons ago, flooded her mind. They were memories of a different time when she felt she had the world by the tail and anything she might want was hers for the asking, a time of false illusions of safety and control. "Stan?" she asked, forcing herself to come back to the present.

"That's right. It's been a while since we talked, hasn't it?"

Tessa thought two weeks but she didn't voice her thoughts aloud. "So what's up?" she asked instead. How did you find my phone number? she thought actually. Her phone number was unlisted. He'd certainly never called her before.

"Surprised, Tessa? I was looking over your therapy chart from last year when that leg started acting up again and thought I'd give you a call."

Of course, the chart. Her phone number was on that. "So what's—be careful," she called out to the freezer men who were now moving her table to make more room. Good heavens!

"Careful?" Stan's voice came across the

line confused before his rich chuckle sounded. ''That's Tessa.''

With a chuckle, he continued speaking. ''I wanted to tell you, I just moved to Hill Creek.'' She heard someone in the background say something to Stan. He paused and replied. Then he was back talking to her. ''We'll talk when I get over there.''

Tessa, who had been shifting from foot to foot with worry over the way the beefy men had handled her table, became suddenly alert at Stan's words. ''I'm sorry?'' *Here?* she thought.

Moving around the corner of the doorway, blocking out the disaster going on in her kitchen, she tuned all of her energy to the man on the phone. ''Run that by me again, Stan?''

''I moved to Hill Creek. And since I come so highly qualified, the attending physician has assigned me as nurse to the man moving into your house. I'll be seeing you every morning.''

Stunned, Tessa sank to a footstool in front

of a recliner chair in her living room. "You're here, in Hill Creek?"

"That's right. Isn't it great?"

Tessa simply shook her head. Five years ago she'd been in love with a man named Michael—or she thought she'd been in love with him. He'd been so upbeat just like Stan, so outgoing, so forward in his pursuit. Then the earthquake had come, her injuries had come, and they'd broken up. She'd broken up. He'd broken up with her. It was all too much to think about right now. He'd sworn he still cared for her and just needed time to adjust to their new circumstances. But it hadn't been the truth. It'd been her, the emptiness that had run him off.

He didn't want her. She couldn't live with all of the pain that had been running through her after the horrible earthquake and loss. The only good thing that had happened during that time was that she'd rededicated herself to God. That had changed her life. She had wanted to put all of the past behind her. She'd *tried* to put the past behind her. She had realized after rededicating her heart to God that she couldn't stay there and watch her former fiancé marry and set up practice in her town of Brea.

So she'd packed up and left. She'd tried once or twice to date. She'd met Stan, who had seemed like such a nice man. Kind, gentle, funny…but she just hadn't been able to risk it.

"Tessa, you still there?"

But if she read this one right, he was interested in more than therapy. Tessa nodded, then realizing he couldn't see her answered, "Yes. That's um, great, Stan, that you're here."

Stan chuckled. "I've been in town two weeks now. I live out west, on the other side of the hospital, but I saw you at the school, just before it let out. And you wouldn't believe the way small towns are. I think I've heard everything about you and every other single person that lives in this Podunk town in those two weeks. I'd been waiting to contact you… Anyway, we'll catch up later. I just thought I'd call and let you know I'm back."

"Thanks, Stan. It's good to hear your voice." She meant that, in a way. In another way she didn't. She wasn't sure what to say to him. She remembered in the hospital when he'd worked on the therapy, the lasting result from the earthquake that flared up occasionally. She'd really enjoyed his company, maybe because he was so nice, did most of the talking, and showed such enthusiasm.

But when he'd wanted to walk her home and then sent her those cards...it was too reminiscent of her past with Michael.

He hung up.

Tessa replaced the receiver as well. Stan now lived in town.

What was she going to do? She toyed with the idea of dating him. He certainly was persistent. And he even attended the same church she did when he was in town on a Sunday— which wasn't often. He had the time to spend with her.

She'd spent weeks in the hospital five years earlier when the earthquake had collapsed the building she was in. It was during that time she'd been told she would never have children—it was impossible from all the damage. That had devastated her, but Michael... Michael hadn't been able to handle it at all.

After Michael broke off their engagement Tessa headed east, stopping in Hill Creek, Texas, where they had been seeking teachers. She had not kept in touch with many people—only one or two through occasional letters.

She hadn't been able to date since. Twice men had found out about her infertility and had stopped calling. Stan was the first man who had shown an interest in her since then. Oh, she'd gone out with Mitch, entertaining the idea of maybe marrying the nice man. He was a sheriff and would provide safety. He was nice, quiet. But on that one date they hadn't clicked. She'd actually wanted to leave from the time they'd entered the restaurant. It had been more than obvious to her that their waitress, Suzi, was in love with Mitch.

After that, she had resigned herself to being an old maid. But Stan was in town now. How interesting.

Worry made her bite her lip. She realized she was being silly since he probably only wanted to be a friend.

She stood and moved to go check on the puppy, wishing she could just forget the past and go on with the life she'd started here. She'd only taken two steps when she noticed her kitchen. Her mind went absolutely blank with shock. *"Oh good heavens!"*

Not only had a freezer been moved into her abode but they had totally reworked the stairs out back and they were just finishing the door. "What are you doing?"

"Wheelchair accessible, ma'am," a new person said.

"This is my house!" she protested.

The ramp had obviously already been built and was simply being laid over her stairs and secured with railing. It was a long, slow incline, which meant it took up a large part of her walk. "Orders—"

"—ma'am," she finished, then gasped when she realized they must have moved things around out back as well so they could put up the ramp. "I have turtles mating out there!"

"We moved them," the carpenter said as if that answered everything.

"Where?" she asked, counting to ten. What had she let Freckles get her into? Her animals were in utter chaos. Her life was suddenly in utter chaos!

"Over in that round pond thing you have."

Groaning she scooted past the men and hurried outside and down the ramp. She snatched up the turtles from the pond and set them out in another part of the yard. "This just isn't going to do. What do they think they're doing? Why are they destroying my house like this?" Tessa leaned down to retrieve another turtle.

"Do you always talk to yourself?"

The slightly slurred words caught Tessa's attention. Peeking between her knees she saw a wheelchair and two sets of boots behind her. The feet in the chair had on dead snake boots, she noted distastefully, and a dark pair of jeans.

Realizing she was in shorts and giving the

man a good view of her behind she dropped the turtles. Whirling, she met the gaze of the man in the wheelchair.

So this was Drake Slater. The man was thin, very thin—too thin for a person of his height. His face was white, indicating it'd been a while since he'd been out in the sun. His head had a huge scar on it, the hair just starting to grow out over the ugly pink-and-white spot. Down the entire right side of his face and neck, disappearing into his striped blue shirt, was a mass of thin, healing scars.

''Barbed wire.''

Realizing she was staring, she again met the gaze of the man in the chair. Deep green eyes filled with intelligence, though his right eye and a small bit of the right side of his mouth drooped, stared steadily back. She found she couldn't break eye contact.

It wasn't until one of the men dropped a hammer that she realized she was staring utterly dumbfounded. Those eyes had such a...strength...a...a... ''Hello...Mr. Slater?''

The mouth stretched into a caricature of a

grin. "You always have men coming to your door in chairs?"

She blushed furiously. Why she wasn't sure. This man was in a wheelchair, for pity's sake. She was in charge of this situation, not him. So why did his words have her blushing like he was the first man she'd met? But those eyes…a wealth of emotion shone in them. It was like he looked in her and knew what she was thinking.

No one had ever done that before.

"Ahem."

Glancing past the ruffling black hair, Tessa realized the second set of boots belonged to a younger version of the man in the chair. Black hair, green eyes but instead of thin and emaciated, this man looked strong, ready to take on what life handed him—including her if his look of disapproval was any indication.

"Do you always walk around looking like a pirate, Miss Stanridge?"

She blinked at the younger Slater brother. "Excuse me?"

"Thaaat's enough, Le-um," Drake warned his brother mildly. Tessa remembered Freckles saying when he was upset or nervous he slurred his words. Her gaze snapped to his. His look traveled over her briefly, the corners of his mouth twitching just before he burst out laughing.

Liam gaped. So did Tessa for that matter.

"I like your bird," Drake finally said.

Oh good heavens, Tessa thought, her cheeks heating up again.

Sam squawked.

She'd forgotten the bird was on her shoulder. Weakly she smiled. "They're rearranging my kitchen. Sam was upset and wanted to be held."

"Can I?"

Tessa hesitated, then thought she might as well let him try. Lifting her forearm, she signaled Sam with her index and middle fingers. The bird obediently stepped up onto the back of her hand. "He really doesn't like other people, Mr. Slater...."

"Draeg..."

"Drake," she nodded.

"Please."

She met his eyes. In those eyes were not

only intelligence but gentleness and need. She wasn't sure what he needed but it was there in his eyes. Without another word, she held out the bird, which transferred itself onto his shoulder. She silently vowed at that moment to stop staring at this man. She was certain she wasn't making a good impression with Liam. Look at the sky, she told herself, then argued that'd be rude.

His words interrupted her thoughts.

"Wow."

Her gaze went to him. His eyes sparkled with pleasure and his teeth showed when he smiled. Grinning devilishly up at her, he winked. "Pirate."

She found herself returning his grin. "Sam doesn't take to others well."

His gaze met hers. "He must like me."

Tessa thought this man was reading her thoughts again.

"You really shouldn't do that, Drake," Liam cut in, spoiling the smile on Drake's face. "What if he bites those scars or scratches you up more?"

Drake sighed impatiently.

The bird, picking up Drake's sudden tension, squawked and started dancing.

Tessa scooped up the bird, wincing when he dug in his claws.

"Thank you—" Liam began.

"Why don't we go inside," Tessa offered. "Your brother is looking tired."

Drake scowled at them both. What had happened to the smile the man had just worn? Where had it gone?

"Which way?" Liam asked.

Tessa took that as her cue and went back up the ramp, which the carpenter was just finishing. Even with her back to Drake, the spell over her emotions was still in full force. She wondered if there was such a thing as meeting someone who you just knew was going to play an important part of your life—like God saying, look here, don't miss this. He's important to you.

If so, then Tessa was certain that was what just happened to her. She didn't know how or why but this man... She had met her destiny in some way or another.

In Your hands, Father, she silently prayed, giving Him control in this situation. She had learned what she didn't understand and couldn't control she had to allow God to control. She saw a young woman come out of her kitchen and head toward a gray van on the side of the house, in which Liam must have just arrived.

"That's Kellie, the cook. She's a great girl. She cooks for us out at the ranch. Her mother cooked there before she did," Liam said.

Tessa nodded at his words. The young Hispanic woman was beautiful, Tessa thought, but didn't say so. Instead, she continued up the ramp and into the house.

"We're worried about infection so I hope you keep a clean house," Liam said now.

Tessa glanced around, surprised. "I would think you'd have checked all of that out before you agreed to let me be a keeper."

Drake growled. It startled Tessa. She thought at first he was choking, until she caught the anger in his eyes. "I don't need a keeper."

Liam scowled at her then tried to soothe his brother. "Yes. You do. You still aren't well enough to come home. Tessa will be working with you as will your nurse, and Kellie will be here to cook for you. Soon, Drake, you'll be well enough to boss me around again." To Tessa's ears Liam didn't sound like he really believed that, though.

Drake shoved at his brother's hand, his look downright dark.

Oh dear. She couldn't help but feel she was back in the schoolroom with a group of rowdy third graders as she watched the two brothers interact. Taking a breath she decided it might be best to break up the tension before it got any worse.

Crossing the kitchen she reached for the door to the bedroom. In a bright voice, she said, much like a Realtor trying to sell a man seeking a simple abode the house of his dreams, "This room right here is where Drake will be staying. It has its own facilities. There's an outside door." She paused, listening. "As a matter of fact, I think I hear the carpenter working on the entrance right now."

Glancing around she realized suddenly that Drake's chair wouldn't fit through the area between the sink and the table. "I see we're going to have to make some adjustments," she said, laughing nervously when she realized the way the table was positioned wouldn't allow him to get into the living room. ''We'll work all of this out. Let's look at your room first, shall we?'' she continued, simply wanting the tension in the room to ease.

She pushed the door open, smiling at them. Instead of smiles, however, the two gaped past her. Slowly, in unison, two green-eyed stares turned to her, tension still very evident in the stunned looks.

''What?'' she asked. Surely they didn't hate the room. This was one of her favorite rooms. It was like a playroom for her. She had decorated it herself. Hardly anyone ever stayed in it so time and again she found herself going by an antique store and picking up some cute piece of furniture or knickknack to add. It was quite a nice room.

Or it had been. When she turned her head to point out the features she found herself gaping, too, just before she burst out with, ''Oh my heavens!''

Disaster had struck the formally picturesque room. The beautiful blue, green and yellow quilt, which had covered the bed, straggled off the end of the four-poster at an odd angle, trailing onto the floor. The tiny lace pillows, which had lain on top, now decorated the braided carpet. The small throw rug she had positioned in front of the dresser was no longer there. Instead, it curled up crazily against the far, papered wall. But the worst thing she could see that had happened to the room was the toilet paper. It adorned everything. At least everything that was within leaping distance for a small puppy. The chair, the small nightstand, the bed all had their share of adornment.

And where was the perpetrator of the mess?

In the middle of a box of tissues was Hubert, his tongue lolling out. He yipped at the new arrivals and then went back to tearing up the carton.

The loud burst of laughter from Drake encouraged her, until she heard him say, "Great going, brother. I have a keeper, all right. A zoo keeper."

Chapter Three

Drake couldn't believe everything that had just happened in his short time in this strange household. He'd been going insane in the hospital. Between the looks from the doctors and the people who had come to visit and the worry from his brother, he'd been certain they were going to pray him right into a grave.

They had no hope for him. Each look they had given him had made him all the more determined to prove to them he could live. Live for what, he didn't know. He had no idea. As badly torn up as he was from the barbed wire and the damage that bull had done to his head, Drake was certain he'd never be much good at anything again.

He'd had a cerebral hemorrhage, they'd told him, from all the damage. But that had been minor compared to what the bull had done to him. It was a miracle he'd lived, they told him. They couldn't believe he was making progress at all, they'd say. The darkness that had settled on him from all of the negative comments and looks in the hospital had been nearly debilitating at times.

The only one who hadn't been gloom and doom had been Dr. Susan McCade and her husband, called Dr. Hawk in affectionate terms by his wife. Dr. Susan would look in on Drake, it seemed, and know what to say. She made him smile. She'd been the only person in that forsaken place that had been able to do that. But this Stanridge woman had, in just a few short minutes, accomplished that and more. He felt alive again.

Liam tried to pretend as if nothing was the matter, that in no time Drake would be well. However, it was his fearful looks that he wasn't suppose to see that made Drake feel like he was on death's door.

When Liam had told him he wanted to move Drake to a house for recuperation and training, Drake had been in total disagreement. The way things had gone so far, he didn't want to take any more advice that anyone might give him. After all, if Liam really thought he was going to die, just what type of place might those others suggest for Drake? The only thing that made him agree to try was that Dr. Susan McCade assured him she had made the arrangements and that his brother really was worried only like a little brother might be. Besides, he really couldn't argue with someone who had access to the phone, truck and outside contacts like his brother did.

He supposed throwing the tray at that nurse when she'd brought him that latest batch of pills had been what had decided this move. But he was restless. He wanted to do more than they would allow.

He was over the pneumonia that had complicated things and was functioning again...

somewhat. He was angry and frustrated that he could look at words and have no idea what they said, whereas a few months ago he could have read them. Now, they didn't make the least bit of sense.

Drake wasn't an idiot. And he hadn't been kidding the first few times Liam had brought him something to read. He couldn't understand it. He was determined to relearn how to read and write and especially how to walk again. Supposedly only the doctor, Liam and Drake knew what was going on here—that this woman had agreed not only to let him stay close to the hospital, but to teach him the rest of the time. It was humiliating. It had been, at least. Until the woman had peeked between her legs at him, the bird hanging on to her shoulder upside down, his beak grasping her hair like he was certain his life was over if he let go.

When she'd turned around, her face red, her cheeks flushing with her embarrassment and not even realizing that the bird was unraveling the lace around her shirt, he couldn't help but laugh.

For that short time he'd forgotten he was an invalid, that he couldn't read, that he looked like a cross between Frankenstein and Dracula.

For that short time he'd felt like a man again, noticing the shapely curve of the woman's legs, the way her brown wavy hair bounced around her face as she had turned to face him. And the way those piercing blue eyes had studied him.

Then he'd realized she was staring at his scars. It'd all come painfully back to him.

And if his brother said one more thing about his condition he was going to get out of the chair and show him just who was still the boss.

Keeper indeed. The woman had a lot to learn, he thought sourly. Still, he couldn't resist a crack about the golden little puppy. "I hope you don't expect the lion king there to share my room with me."

"Oh dear," she said very low, so low he almost missed it. "No. Of course not. It's been um, a busy morning. I have to...that is...you can sleep in the cook's room and I'll get this cleaned up and then we'll move you in here later. How's that?''

He watched her hurry over and shove the table out of the way, making room for his chair to slip through into the next room—the living room, from what he could see sitting where he was.

Drake heard Liam's phone ring and heard him answer it, but he didn't take his gaze off the woman's attempts to put things right.

As she moved back and forth, shoving a chair here, moving a footstool there, he saw another cage past the door with something running around in it. The old wooden boards of the floor lacked a polish but were sturdy just the same and echoed her hurried steps loudly.

He heard his brother say something about calling the vet and then hang up. ''Another cow sick. I have to go, Drake. I'll call this evening and if you want I'll find you somewhere a bit more sane.''

Tessa had slipped into the living room and continued shoving her furniture around, making sure he had room to get through. Watching her he slowly shook his head. "If I need a keeper, here is as good a place as any."

Liam sighed. "It wasn't meant like that, Drake. We're all worried. You've recovered so quickly that if you go back out to the ranch I'm afraid—the *doctors* are afraid—you'll have a relapse. Just consider this a halfway house of recovery."

Drake nodded. "And I am going to recover, Liam."

Liam hesitated. "Of course you are," he finally said.

Drake clenched his fists. "God is in control," he whispered.

Liam didn't say anything. He didn't believe in God. And Drake hadn't told him that he thought he'd seen an angel as the bull had hit him. In that split second, his life had changed. In that moment he realized that God was real, that He did care. God had saved him from his past transgressions, had given him hope…and a new life.

Drake didn't understand why but he did believe God had saved him from certain death.

"Why didn't He save you from this then?"

Liam asked quietly. Before Drake could reply, he added, "I've got to go."

And that was that. Liam walked out on him.

"Oh!" Tessa said coming back. "He's gone. Well, let's go see the rest of the house, shall we? Kellie? Make yourself at home. I was going to put you in the main room but Hubert has made a mess of Mr. Slater's room. So I'm going to put him in there, okay?"

"Sí, *señorita*," she said, and started unloading dishes.

"Dishes?" Tessa asked, her voice rising a bit.

Kellie grinned. "I have my favorite dishes to cook with. I hope you do not mind I bring my own."

Put that way, what could Tessa say? "Of course not. If anyone comes to the door while I'm settling Mr. Slater, would you please handle them?"

"Of course, Miss Stanridge."

"Drake. How hard is that to remember?" he muttered to the woman as she started steering him through the quaint little house. The

tapestry on the floor was thin with age, probably having come with the house, Drake
thought, glancing at it as she wheeled him
over it and past a rolltop desk.

The furniture looked old and worn in, comfortable, lived in, he thought, unlike the
newer furniture they had in his house.

"Right now you'll have to share the bath-
room with the rest of us. It's down this hall
here. Under the stairs. My room is upstairs.
The other room down this hall is the catchall
room. Uninhabitable."

He saw a toad, two turtles, a hamster and
a lizard.

Yes, he thought, doing a double take of the
monster that walked across the floor into the
catchall room, which was certainly a lizard—
of some sort. "You like animals," he commented.

Tessa chuckled. "Oh, my yes. That's my
hobby. I collect them. Fix them up and even-
tually let them go, except for my pets."

"Is the lizard a pet?" He couldn't help but
ask.

"Alfred? Oh, well, I baby-sit him. A

trucker down the street—Mr. McHugh—he and his daughter truck together and when they're gone they need someone to watch Alfred. It's usually a couple of weeks a month. But Alfred is well behaved. You don't have to worry about him.''

''Just the dog?''

She chuckled. He liked the way the woman laughed. He'd never met Tessa Stanridge before. He didn't have children. He'd been told she was one of the new teachers at their local elementary school. She and two others had come to Hill Creek in the last few years. The town was growing.

Hard to believe, but it was. More and more people were moving out here. Escaping the big city, he supposed. The one he used to fly to every couple of weeks.

Until his accident.

He liked the way the woman smelled, too. She didn't smell like alcohol and soap or of sterile hospital equipment. She smelled fresh and...earthy. She swayed as she walked. She didn't have that brisk walk like the one a nurse or doctor had.

She wasn't all business.

She was pleasure.

The joy in her eyes, the way her cheeks turned pink, the way she stopped to say a word to each animal she passed, that soft gentle voice. It soothed him.

"Again, Mr. Sla—Drake, I have to apologize. I'm normally more organized...."

He doubted that.

"...but today with the people delivering everything and all... I just put the puppy in there so he wouldn't trip the men. I didn't even think about him tearing anything up. He's still a puppy."

"Yeah," he agreed. Still a puppy. When was the last time he'd noticed a puppy? When was the last time he'd taken time to notice any animal?

Shaking his head, he said, "I suppose."

It'd been too long. He didn't remember how puppies acted. He and his brother had one as children. But that'd been a long time ago.

"Here we go. This is your room."

It was a nice room, too. Once again the

floor was wooden with a threadbare rug covering part of it. A four-poster spindle bed with a pink patchwork quilt took up the biggest part of the room. A lacy cloth covered the old-fashioned dresser along with different knickknacks.

It looked like a woman's room. "Does the cat come with the room?" he asked, nodding toward the armoire where the cat lay on top.

Walking around him, Tessa laughed and crossed to scoop up the animal. "I'm afraid Missy comes with whatever she wants. Missy rules here. I hope you aren't allergic?"

He shook his head. "Not that I've noticed."

Relief shone in her eyes. "Good. Missy has always been with me. She goes with me everywhere but has a mind of her own. The rest of the animals I'll try to keep out of your way, Drake. But Missy…"

Drake felt obligated to say something. "It's your house. You're helping me. I appreciate that, Miss…"

"Call me Tessa."

"Tessa." He nodded. The name was a bit

hard to pronounce but he would get it down He'd practice tonight and learn it.

She smiled. He saw her glance at the scars again. "How much help will you need getting around here, Drake? Freckles didn't tell me exactly how incapacitated you were."

He frowned. Reaching slowly down he locked the sides of the chair. "Come here," he said softly.

She hesitated, then set the cat down, and came forward. He motioned her to his right side and then slowly, very slowly stood.

"Walk with me to the bed."

She obeyed.

He wanted to rage at the way his right leg still dragged along the floor some, the way his arm wasn't under his complete control. Instead, he thanked God he was alive. Whenever it got him down, he forced himself to remember he could have died without ever knowing God loved him.

But he hadn't died.

Making it to the bed he turned and finally sat down. "If you help me get my leg up, I can get it down much easier. It just cuts the time in half.''

''Oh.'' Leaning down, she helped him lift his leg.

Feeling exhausted, he nodded. ''That's all the help I need, Tessa,'' he said carefully, frowning over how garbled her name had sounded.

She smiled. ''Good. Well, do you want to go back in or, um, rest?''

Drake sighed. ''This is awkward for you, isn't it?''

She shrugged. ''It certainly is different.''

He offered her a smile. ''For me, too. I'll tell you what. Let's just be open and honest with each other and commu...coom...talk and it'll work out.''

She didn't blush at his stumbling over the word ''communicate.'' He'd seen more than one of his friends do that. Get over it, he wanted to say. But when it still frustrated him, how could he tell another person to get over it?

''Very well. I'll tell you what I think. My mother had a stroke. You look like she did when she'd done too much and was exhausted.''

He nodded. "I am that."

"Then what if you sleep until Kellie or I wake you for dinner?"

He grinned. Listening to the authority in her voice and the way she didn't start catering to him and fluttering over him made him decide they were going to get along just fine. "That sounds good."

Relief colored her features and she grinned. "Great. In the meantime, I have some rabbits I have to check on and a kitchen and living room to get back in order. And then we'll make sure your suitcase gets in here."

Going to the window, she pulled the drapes. She then moved his chair closer. At the armoire she pulled out a sheet and handed it to him. After taking off his boots, she covered him.

He scowled.

She grinned. "Sorry. There. Now I'll go and you can rest. I'll leave the door open. Call out if you need anything."

How had she known what he was thinking? "I'll do that."

She walked out of the room, pulling the door nearly shut behind her so that she could hear if he called out. She'd forgotten Missy, he noted, when the cat jumped up and curled against his legs, coming to rest near his side.

Reaching out with his left hand, he stroked the cat. "Well, Missy, you've accepted me. I wonder how much your owner has?"

When the cat meowed, he smiled and closed his eyes thinking he'd find out soon enough. In the meantime, he was going to enjoy the peace and quiet.

Chapter Four

And he'd thought the hospital had been noisy with the constant paging of nurses and administrative types. That or the sound of metal against metal as dishes were handed out and gathered up, or nurses laughing and chatting at three different times—including eleven at night and around six-thirty in the morning.

Still, somehow he'd adjusted to that noise. But this...

"A-a-a-ck. Br-a-a-t Bird. Wake up! A-a-a-ck!"

The shrill whistle of the "1812 Overture"

in his ear snapped his eyes open. Jerking his head toward the sound, he came face-to-beak with the offending creature. Lifting its wings, the parrot bobbed its head. "A-a-ck, br-a-a-t wake up!"

"No, no!" Tessa came hurrying into the room, arms full of a fluff ball that had to be a rabbit. The long floppy white-and-pink ears confirmed it. Just how many more animals did this woman have? he had to wonder.

When she realized he was awake, she sighed. "Shame on you, Sam. Go back to your perch."

"Br-a-at bird," the parrot muttered, his head bobbing in what looked like an abject apology to his owner. What was amazing, however, was that the bird obeyed.

Sam jumped down to the ground and started across the floor toward the door.

"You trained it?" Drake asked, working to make his right leg slide over the edge of the bed.

She shook her head. "Not completely. A former pet-shop owner taught him the saying you just heard and how to whistle. Believe it or not, most birds learn one or the other.''

Managing to get to a sitting position, Drake nodded. ''Lucky for us he knows both.''

Her chuckle drew a reluctant grin from him. ''He's quite smart. Kellie?''

Only then did Drake see the cook at the door. ''Hello, Kellie.''

''Mr. Slater,'' the woman said softly and offered him a quick smile.

''Kellie, can you take the rabbit for me? I need to help Drake up,'' Tessa said.

''Of course.'' Coming forward, Kellie accepted the rabbit and spoke softly in her native language to calm the furry little beast.

Tessa moved up next to the bed and reached out to assist him into his chair. He noticed she'd changed. Instead of the shorts and dirt she'd worn earlier, she had donned a stretchy pair of olive leggings with a huge white cotton shirt over them. Small shoes encased her feet.

With her hair pulled up in a ponytail as it was, she could easily pass for a kid herself. No wonder the school kids loved this woman.

She related to them. And yet there was something completely woman about her, too. The curve of her cheek, the gentle movement of her hands that looked nearly musical in the way they moved with such grace.

He allowed the tiny Tessa to slip her arm around him and brace herself as he struggled up. Turning, he lowered his body until it met the chair. Moving stiffly, he settled himself into the wheeled menace. "I really don't want to use this much."

"I understand," Tessa said, shooting him a look of empathy. The understanding in her eyes made him wonder if she had ever been in a chair like this.

She didn't elaborate, though. Instead, she continued with her sentence. "However, let's utilize it before meals. You need your strength to eat. Then, after meals, if the nurse agrees, we'll let you wander wherever you want."

"Awfully free with your rez…home, aren't you? Offering me your entire house," he murmured.

He could hear the smile in her voice as she

pushed him into the living room. "Ah, but I know you can't get around very well yet, so what am I losing in offering you that?"

Astonished, he simply gaped. Then he chuckled. "My brother wouldn't have said that to me."

"Family does have a tendency to worry overly much."

"Yes," he said. "Even when you try to explain that God is in control."

He waited for her reaction. It wasn't long in coming. "Do you go to church, Drake?"

Somehow, that wasn't what he had expected her to ask. He was still shining inside with the newness of his discovery. Asking if you went to church seemed so...so...not right. "No. I don't."

"Oh."

"Do you?" he asked back, figuring he might as well since she hadn't asked what he'd wanted her to ask.

"Well, yes. Actually, I do." Pushing him over near the sofa, she parked the wheelchair and then sat down. Picking up a book, she opened it, then glanced at him. "Are you a Christian, Drake?"

He shrugged. Well, there was the question he'd hoped for. So why did he feel embarrassed or pushy wanting to tell her? Unable to help himself, he smiled at her and confessed anyway. "Yeah."

She returned his gentle smile. "I am as well. I take it, however, you haven't been long."

If that wasn't an invitation to tell her his story, then he wasn't sure what was. He wanted to talk to someone, anyone, who believed. His brother didn't and thought he was crazy. The nurses said it was a miracle he was alive but if he tried to explain how he really felt it was a miracle, they avoided him like he'd lost what little of his brain he had left.

It'd been frustrating trying to find someone, anyone, to talk with about his new experiences. But this woman— Well, hopefully he'd found someone. She had said she believed.

I hope she does, God, he said silently, and then with a deep breath he plunged ahead.

"I've heard the message of God a lot, but I just never really felt it applied to me—or that it was for today." He talked slowly so she could understand him. He appreciated the way she listened in return.

"Many people don't," Tessa agreed.

"I know God did things in the old days, when Jesus was around. But that has faded. Does that make sense?"

"It wasn't real to you?" she asked gently.

Thinking how long he had been without God, he nodded. "Yeah. It wasn't real. I mean, every religion has their own way. To each his own. Tolerance and all—just don't push that stuff off on me, you know. But lately, in the last few months I kept questioning…is this all there is to life? Isn't there anything more?" He paused to catch his breath and regroup. Talking this much, he found, was a tiring experience. "Life was filled with nothing. You earned money, you worked, but that was it. Soon you'd die and then nothing."

"What changed that?"

Drake hesitated. He didn't know how much

he should tell her. So he skirted the most intimate parts. "I was out riding on the range. There were things that needed to be done and it was my responsibility.... Anyway, I was thinking, wondering just what God had to offer the world, why this God was so real to some while to others He wasn't. I even wondered why someone could believe in someone they'd never seen. I mean, you have it all over...these people believing in gods. I had caught a short piece of one of those religious shows...but the guy had something to say about there being one true God who really cared.

"I'd always thought that was rhetoric until I heard this guy. He really made it sound real.

"Anyway, I was asking God if He was there and supposedly cared about us, why He'd let my cattle get so sick. There's been a recent outbreak of problems with our cattle, you understand."

Wiping a hand across his head he adjusted his body as best he could. Tessa got up and helped. When he was ready, she was there to listen. "Right in the middle of this question my horse shied. He saw what I'd missed…a snake out on a casual stroll. With my mind on other things, I wasn't prepared. My horse threw me.'' He could feel the dull red creep onto his cheeks by admitting that.

He'd been riding way too long to let something so silly nearly cost him his life. "I almost got killed all because of a snake."

"I thought it was barbed wired and…"

Drake shook his head. "No. I was out checking the cattle—especially the bull. I hit hard, falling into the barbed wire. The bull got me while I was down."

Tessa gasped.

Drake nodded grimly. "I don't remember much. I do know while I was down there it seemed as if God wanted to show me how real He was."

Tessa smiled and Drake was almost certain he saw moisture in her eyes. "How?"

Warily he shrugged. This was the part he didn't really want to share. So he told what he could. "When I was down, the bull could have stomped me to death. The snake, which was right there, could have bitten me. My horse could have done any number of things. Instead, I escaped the snake. The bull, I do know he ran off suddenly.'' And that's all he'd say about why the bull ran. ''And my horse headed right back to the stables they say, which got me help almost immediately. And while I lay there I realized it took all of that to get my attention and make me look up. I'll tell you, Tessa, had God not been there then, I wouldn't be here now.'' He glanced away, somehow embarrassed to have shared such an intimate story with a near stranger, but again somehow feeling as if he'd done the right thing. He figured it must have something to do with what he'd heard about everyone being relatives in God.

''That's a beautiful story, Drake.''

Glancing carefully at her, he asked, ''How long…?''

She understood what he wanted. ''I was raised in church. I gave my life to God at a young age, but as I grew older, I got bored with the ritual of it all. I didn't see any big deal about it either.'' She smiled and patted his hand. "I almost lost my life in an earthquake. Things like that can change a person."

He nodded. He wanted to hear more but had a feeling that was all she wanted to say so he changed the subject. "Has my brother called?"

Tessa nodded. "I was out when he did. Kellie said some more problems with the cattle have cropped up and he won't be in tonight. Oh, and your nurse said to tell you he'd be here first thing in the morning."

An awkward silence fell. He could hear Kellie making dinner, smell the spicy aromas. Finally, Tessa cleared her throat.

"You said we should be up front with each other."

He nodded.

"I don't know you well, Drake, but if we're going to have a working relationship, then I think we should discuss what your brother wants."

"What I want," he corrected.

She nodded. "What you want."

He waited.

"Tell me what you see when you pick up a book."

"Greek."

She blinked. "Excuse me? I'm afraid I didn't quite understand that. I mean, of course, I understood it but…"

He'd confused her. It was obvious from the odd look on her face. Of course, he didn't mean he actually saw Greek. Sighing he explained, "Some words make perfect sense while others just don't *fit*."

"You understand some of them?"

"I understand *all* of them. I just can't *read* them all."

Tessa sighed and guilt immediately assailed him.

"That's not what I meant," she apologized quietly.

"I realize that, Miss…"

"Tessa."

"Tessa."

"Let's try again." Getting up, she crossed the room and opened a cabinet revealing shelves full of books. Pulling down a thin child's reader Tessa returned to his side.

Opening it, she pointed to the first page. "What does this say?"

He looked at the blue-and-red drawing and the picture of the pig. Staring at it, he worked hard. He tried sounding it out and got part of it. But some of the words...

Frustration built. This was a book any child could read. Yet, staring at it, he couldn't make out half the words. Anger and frustration warred within him. He slapped the book away. "I should know that!" he growled in frustration. "It's a kid's book!"

Reaching out, Tessa caught his arm. Her heart ached for him. Deep green eyes filled with frustration reached out and wrapped around her heart, pulling her into their depths. Holding on to his hand, she waited until he looked at her, calmer. "You do know it," she said softly, smiling at him. "You just can't read it."

Watching the effect of having his words repeated back to him, she couldn't help but release a huge sigh of relief at his smile. "Trickery," he murmured out in a slight slur.

Slowly, she shook her head. "The truth.

Since Dr. McCade told me about your case, I've been doing some research. I like research. Anyway, the knowledge is all there, Drake. It's just locked up where we can't get to it. Give your brain time to grow around and reteach other areas. You've got plenty of extra room up there,'' she said, motioning toward his head, ''that can learn. Also, Dr. McCade told me she has a feeling you're going to learn a lot more than anyone else thinks. It has to do with your blind stubbornness.''

He smiled. ''She believes in me.''

Amazingly enough, in the short time Tessa had known him, she had to agree. Holding on to the rough, calloused hand that was so big and yet so gentle, she smiled. ''I do, too. You're strong and determined and we'll teach you how to read. But first, let me tell you, kids books aren't that bad. The pictures and words together will help you learn. And don't worry. As we go through those, you'll pick up the words quickly.''

''What if I don't?''

Tessa hesitated. She'd been trying to sound

encouraging, but there was the possibility that he wouldn't relearn everything. Glancing past him, she said, "God chooses the unlearned to confound the wise?"

He chuckled. "Not nice to say to a learned man who's had this problem."

She returned his smile. "But the truth. Sometimes we don't understand what happens to us or why." She couldn't help but think about the earthquake so many years ago and all of the ensuing damage. "But, God can still use us if we let Him use us."

"In other words, if I don't learn it, I'll still be a valuable asset to society."

She shrugged. "I don't know about society. But you will be to God."

Strangely enough, that comforted him. "My brother would fire you right now if he heard you say that."

"I wouldn't say that to your brother," she said grinning cheekily. Realizing she still held his hand, she abruptly let it go.

"Oh?"

She couldn't believe how open she was with this man, how honest. But he demanded that of her. His simple words, his open honesty would allow nothing else. He was the strangest man she'd ever met. Looking into his eyes, seeing the way he stared so intently, she said, "Your brother is still too scared he's going to lose you for me to say something like that. Tell me," she said abruptly, reaching out to touch his cheek, "does it hurt?"

The warmth of his skin and gentle brushing of his beard sent shivers down her spine. Her eyes widened and shot to his.

He had the strangest look on his face. "Not when you touch it," he murmured.

"Dinner," Kellie called.

Tessa pulled her hand back. "I have a feeling you were a flatterer before the accident. Come on, let's go eat."

Drake shook his head. "That doesn't matter anymore. With the way I look, the shape I'm in, I won't have to worry about a woman giving me a second look again."

Tessa heard the note of discouragement in his voice and had to admit he might be right. Even though she found the spirit of this man something she hadn't expected, she feared most women wouldn't look past the outward scars.

Most women would consider him a beast.

Chapter Five

"She certainly is a beauty," Liam said to Drake, while sitting out in the yard with his brother.

Glancing at his brother, he saw immediately where this was going. "She's a Christian," Drake warned.

Liam scowled. "Well, at least you're safe. What is it with all of the women being Christians around these parts?"

Drake sighed. "Stan should be here soon."

"Who's Stan?"

"My nurse."

Liam nodded. "Any more visits from Miss Stanridge's herd of animals?"

Drake grinned. "Just a foot-long lizard this morning."

Liam frowned.

Drake shook his head. "Stop worrying, Liam."

"It's my right to worry." Liam stood and crossed over to a blossoming apple tree. "I was supposed to take that run out to check on the cattle but was busy with other pursuits."

Drake's foggy brain did seem to remember that. He wanted to go to his brother, but knew Liam would panic if he left the chair. Instead, he said, "We both were up to chasing women before the accident, Liam. Many times you or I changed off duties if we had something else occupying our time. I don't blame you for this."

Liam turned. "I blame me. Look at you," he said and Drake hurt seeing the pain in his younger brother's eyes. "You're even lucky to be alive. And even if you are alive, are you ever going to be able to function again?"

Darkness descended over Drake at Liam's unintentionally painful words. Pictures of him forever in this chair, pitied by all around, assailed him. It wasn't a pretty sight.

"Drake, it's time for your breakfast."

The sound of Tessa's gentle voice broke into the darkness. Glancing over, he studied her and realized she had probably heard his brother's outburst. She was certainly pretty this morning. The slight color in her cheeks, brown corkscrew curls escaping from the clip that held most of it back. He had to wonder how he'd been so lucky to end up with such an upbeat woman as his teacher and a Christian as well. Seeing the understanding in her eyes gave him an odd strength. Taking a deep breath, he turned to his brother. "I'm alive, Liam. And I thank God for that."

Liam simply shook his head. "I want you back the way you were." Sighing, he ran a hand through his hair. "You deserve better, Drake. Like the old days."

Drake didn't want to think about the old days. He looked back at Tessa and motioned her forward. She moved to his side. "I don't think you were properly introduced yesterday," Drake said and winced at the way his brother's gaze jerked away when he stumbled over the harder words.

Tessa touched his shoulder. Evidently, she had seen the same thing. "I'm Tessa Stanridge." She went forward to shake Liam's hand.

Drake watched his brother shift from guilt mode to trying to get around and reach for her hand.

"You're the younger brother."

"Well, yeah," Liam started.

Tessa interrupted. "I'm sorry we didn't get properly introduced yesterday. It seems Hubert decided to make his pleasure known."

"Hubert?" Liam asked, confused.

Tessa nodded. "The golden shaded puppy you saw. He's part border collie, part who-knows-what."

She chuckled.

Drake smiled at his brother's confusion. Tessa's rattling on and on like that had totally bowled over his baby brother. Liam, who was usually so smooth and in control with women, simply stood gaping at Tessa as she chattered about her animals.

Drake still hadn't decided why the woman had so many animals. He'd watched her during their dinner last night, which had consisted of vegetable soup and bread. She'd constantly paused to talk to one of the animals, or leave the table to check on another of the many other minor disruptions that this woman, constantly in motion, seemed to have.

They were like family to her, he had decided by the time he was ready to retire. Where he had a brother to chat with in the evenings, she had her animals. Or at least, he was thinking that just might be it. So far, he had counted twenty-one separate species in her house. From fish, to frogs, to a snake, all caged and getting proper care. Two people had come to collect their pets yesterday. He thought they were down to around sixteen beasts now. He still wasn't sure.

This was certainly different from the hospital. In a way, he felt like Noah getting ready to embark upon the ark.

"About all of those animals," Liam started.

"About the cows," Drake interrupted.

Liam glanced at his brother.

Kellie interrupted them all. "If you do not come now, Mr. Slater, your breakfast will be cold."

Everyone turned.

Tessa was the first to speak. "Oh my heavens, Kellie. I completely forgot why I came out here!"

Drake chuckled.

Liam grabbed the wheelchair. "That's right. You did mention breakfast, didn't you?"

Tessa watched Liam push his brother toward the ramp into the house. She pondered how nice it was to see Drake laugh. When she'd come out of the house to announce breakfast, Liam had worn an anguished look on his face and Drake's own features had been taut with stress.

His eyes had brooded and his left hand had gripped the wheelchair so tightly that the knuckles were white.

Seeing the glow back in his green eyes and hearing that laugh of his had lightened her heart. Freckles had said it had been a miracle he'd made it and Tessa had a feeling Freckles didn't realize how right she was.

Drake was a breath of fresh air. When he'd struggled last night to tell her the story about his salvation, he had glowed, reminding her of a new child having just discovered their most treasured possession had not been lost but found.

Tessa remembered that feeling from so long ago. His excitement had filled her, making her feel fresh and alive again. How many years now had she just existed—until last night? Five? Or more?

At least that many, she thought.

She had noticed something else, too. When Drake relaxed, his slur wasn't nearly as bad as when he was stressed. He had indeed been working on regaining his muscle coordination. And it looked as if he was making wonderful leaps.

Starting after them she thought of how far he had come. She had only gone two steps when she heard a car out front. Turning, she headed that way instead.

She heard the brothers stop talking, knew they were watching and waiting.

She smiled politely when Stan came around the corner.

Greek god.

They used to joke about that when she had been getting therapy. Tall, athletic and a golden boy, from his shiny sun-blond hair to his skin tone, he reminded her of the sculptures in art books. Square jaw, perfect lips and merry blue eyes, he was the boy next-door and Mr. Universe tied up in one.

"Tessa!" Before Tessa could even say hello, Stan had lunged forward and scooped her up, spinning her around.

Then he kissed her on her forehead—to her utter shock.

He obviously realized she didn't respond as he lowered her to the ground. A curious grin on his face, he said, "Not glad to see me?"

She felt herself flushing to her hairline. She had forgotten what an outrageous teaser he was. When she turned and met the eyes of Drake Slater, she wanted to flush to the bottom of her toes.

His gaze changed from shock, to curiosity, to aloofness. However, seeing Liam's look of sudden interest was what really shook her. "Stan, you know Drake and Liam? We were about ready for breakfast."

Walking over to Drake, she continued, "I've known Stan for a while, since moving to Hill Creek."

"We're pretty close," Stan added, chuckling and winking at Tessa. "I hope I didn't cross the line, Tessa, giving you a welcome kiss like that. I mean, after all, it's not like I haven't…"

"Stan!" she said quietly, rolling her eyes. She hadn't expected that greeting. She didn't want to say anything in front of others but decided to clear the air in front of all of them for Liam's benefit. His look still had her bothered. "Yes, Stan, you did. You're here as Drake's nurse."

Giving her a hurt little boy look he apologized, "I'm sorry, Tessa. You know I sure didn't mean for anything like that to happen."

Drake wondered what was going on,

watching the two. It was obvious from the greeting Stan had given Tessa that they knew each other well. If it had been him, before he was saved, he would have been staking his territory to the other men present.

However, Tessa didn't look at all happy with what Stan had just done as they all trudged up the platform and into the house. Drake wanted to stand up and smack the guy—but because of his problems knew he couldn't.

So what was going on here anyway? he had to wonder.

Stan chose that moment to turn to Drake, just as Liam positioned him in front of the table in the kitchen.

"We're going to work on some muscular development today, Drake. I've brought some small weights along and a list of exercises I want you to do on your own. The rest we'll do together, but the list is something you can do each night to build up body mass."

Drake nodded.

Liam interrupted. "Do you think he's ready for that yet?"

Tessa seated herself across from Drake, leaving the head of the table open for Liam so he could sit next to his brother. Stan slid into the seat next to her. When Kellie started to leave the room, Tessa shook her head. "Join us."

The woman hesitated then nodded, offering her a smile.

Stan noted the byplay and chuckled, then answered Liam's question. "I've trained for many years, Liam. I've worked at countless hospitals and clinics and to be honest, I feel the day you are fully conscious after something like this you should immediately start working on exercises and therapy. Your brother, from what I've read of his case, wasn't started immediately. I would guess, as your doctor told you, that's partially responsible for the pneumonia. However, since his case was so severe there wasn't much choice about what they could do."

"I understand."

"Can we pray?" Tessa cut in.

Stan blinked at her.

Liam shifted uncomfortably.

Drake smiled and bowed his head. Bold little woman, she was.

She said a quick prayer and then picked up her fork. "Go ahead, Stan."

Drake wanted to chuckle at the odd look Stan gave Tessa. "As I was saying," he said before turning his attention back to Liam and Drake, "they got him started and he's made good improvement. With these weights we hope to work that arm and build back some of the atrophied muscle. Also, I want you to start drinking your drinks with a straw."

"Why?" Liam asked before Drake could.

"It's another way to develop the facial muscles. The sucking will help certain muscles that chewing won't. I have other exercises too. I have to warn you, there will probably be days you'll be really angry with me. I do plan to push. I'm a bit unorthodox in my ways, but we want you better."

"Yes," Drake agreed.

Liam shifted uncomfortably but nodded.

Tessa set about eating her pancakes and grits.

Drake watched how Liam and Stan traded

jokes. He wondered just how much harder this nurse could be on him than he'd already been on himself. He wanted to learn. Some nights he was sweating bullets from laying in bed and making his leg move. Each night though, he forced himself to do some sort of exercise to try to build back the muscles and make them work again.

It was the hardest work he'd done in his life.

It put things into perspective, too.

"So, Tessa, tell me, what have you been doing this last year?"

Drake heard the curiosity in Stan's voice and lifted his gaze to gauge Tessa's reaction. He wasn't sure why the question bothered him, but coming from this man, it did.

Tessa laid her fork aside and blotted her lips. "Well, actually, not much. I teach third grade now."

Stan nodded. "I wondered why you were teaching third grade instead of high school."

"I wanted to teach children."

A look of dismay crossed Stan's face. "Well, I can understand that, I suppose. I think you'd be better off teaching older kids. However—'' he shrugged, then relaxed back into his chair ''—it's your life. So, what do you do in your spare time around here?''

Again Tessa glanced at Stan and gave a delicate shrug. ''I have my animals and other hobbies.''

''I saw your bird and dog,'' he said, glancing down at the floor where the dog sat.

''She has other animals as well,'' Liam offered chuckling. ''My brother referred to it as a zoo.''

Stan lifted an eyebrow and studied Tessa. ''Really? Now that's a new hobby.''

She smiled. Drake liked the way her eyes sparkled and her lips curved when she smiled like that. He was afraid he could sit and watch this woman all day, working to memorize every movement. Out of all the women he'd dated in his life, none had captured his attention as this woman had. ''I have a lot of new hobbies,'' she replied to Stan.

''And I can't wait to learn every one of them as I help our patient here. So, Drake,''

Stan said abruptly, turning his attention to him, "are you ready?"

So Stan had noticed he had finished his breakfast, after all. Drake wasn't sure the man had noticed anything but Tessa since arriving. At least he'd been proven wrong there. Wondering where the spurt of possessiveness had come from, he reminded himself Tessa barely knew he existed—especially in the shape he was in right now. Nodding to Stan he said, "Let's go."

He carefully laid his napkin on his plate and waited for Stan to move around the table and push him away. As he left the kitchen, he had to wonder just how things were going to go in the kitchen between Tessa and Liam.

Then he smiled. This third-grade teacher could certainly hold her own.

Tessa stared at Liam, waiting. Kellie stood and quietly left the room. "Was there something you wanted to say to me?"

Liam smiled. "You're very astute."

"I try to be."

"I'm worried about my brother. We need

him near a hospital in case of relapse and this hospital in Hill Creek is the only one for a few hundred miles. I appreciate you opening up your house...."

"But?" she asked.

He sighed. "I don't mean to be rude, Miss Stanridge, but are you sure you are able to handle this? I mean Dr. McCade suggested you..."

Tessa held on to her temper. She imagined this man had every right to ask, and she would do her best to reassure him. "I've never met your brother before, Liam. But I like him. He's fresh and determined. He's wanting to work hard to recover. He has a spirit that few people possess."

"I know that," Liam said, and Tessa heard the anguish in his voice.

Compassion filled her. Reaching out, she touched his hand. "My mother had a stroke, Liam. I'm telling you this because I think it will reassure you. I nursed her, day and night. I was studying to be a nurse at that time. I had a teaching certificate but was burned out on teaching and wanted to do something new.

I quit going to school for it when this happened to my mom. I devoted all of my extra time to nursing her.

"She didn't get better, however. She wanted to die, to go home with my dad. I can tell you that your brother doesn't have a spirit like that. He wants to get better and you can believe I will encourage him in every way I can. As for teaching him to read..." Tessa couldn't help but smile. "I teach third graders. Believe me, if your brother throws a temper tantrum it won't be any worse than what I've already experienced—and handled."

Liam nodded. His cheeks darkened a bit before he cleared his throat. "I have to ask this because of what happened earlier. Will your personal life be interfering with your teaching now that this man is in town?"

Tessa simply lifted a brow. "I don't see why it would. I prefer quiet nights at home. Stan and I aren't dating. We're friends."

Liam shrugged. "I heard you say that but I still worry about my brother."

Tessa nodded. "I understand. And as you are paying the bills here, I can see why you might question me. However, Liam, let me assure you that with Kellie, myself, and his nurse available and Dr. McCade only a phone call away, Drake is going to be just fine."

Liam sighed. "I appreciate your reassurance, Miss Stanridge. Drake gets upset anytime I ask anything."

Patting his hand again, Tessa said, "Perhaps it's because you come off bossy or some other emotion that challenges him as older brother?"

Liam grinned. "I don't know. Drake and I have always been close. But yeah, maybe."

"Give him room. Don't hover. You haven't lost him, Liam."

Liam studied her. Tessa saw the growing admiration in his eyes and hoped that meant she'd won this man over as a friend. "You know, Tessa," Liam finally said, "I think Dr. McCade was right. You are the right person for this job."

She smiled. "Thanks."

"A word of advice from a man?" Liam asked.

"What's that?"

He cocked his head toward the room where Drake and Stan had disappeared. "Stan is interested in you as more than a friend. I don't think he's the type to give up."

"You're an astute man, Liam Slater."

Grinning, he replied, "I try to be."

Chapter Six

"I can't read these. Do you know how ludicrous it sounds for me to read these books?"

Tessa sighed. "Drake, you must understand. These are books that teach you basic words, words you need to learn."

He growled low. "I don't want to read books about Billy or the pig or Polly or little kids and toys. Would you?"

Why had she thought teaching an adult would be easier than working with children? "You want to learn to read?" she questioned, her temper seeping out. "You read these books."

Her formerly sweet if not stubborn student called out, his face set with pure stubborn determination, "Kellie? I want steak cooked rare tonight!"

Tessa gasped.

She'd found out quickly why they needed such a big freezer in the house. Being a vegetarian herself, she hadn't thought about it, until one night he'd had steak.

"You are not going to eat raw meat in my house."

"Make that medium rare, Kellie," he shouted, as if not having any idea what she'd meant.

"Br-r-at man," the bird said and started whistling the "1812 Overture."

The cat, which had been resting on Tessa's lap, hissed and hopped down to get away from the noisy bird.

Hubert started barking at Sam.

The entire house was in chaos simply because this man didn't want to read children's books.

"Not medium rare either!" she warned. "You know what I meant!"

"I'll have my steak if I have to read this stuff."

Tessa growled. After shooing the dog into the other room, she went over, scooped up the happily singing bird and deposited him in the kitchen. If the man dared chuckle, she was going to throw one of the books at him. All morning long he'd been obstinate and determined to do things his way or no way at all.

She was ready to wheel him out back and dump him in the pond.

Taking a deep breath to calm herself, she turned and offered, "What if I find something else for you to read? Will you agree to no more steaks?" The dripping meat had ruined her appetite for the day when Kellie had stood there spicing it. She didn't really want to go through that again. She did see meat—just not raw meat.

"No steaks at all?" He looked aghast at the thought.

She opened her mouth to answer when the cat shot back in, streaking past her. The dog wasn't far behind. "Hubert!"

The dog skidded, hitting the thin tapestry

on the floor and sliding headlong into the coffee table.

"Ha-ha-ha-ha-eck."

Sam was back.

Tessa felt like growling herself. "Sit, Hubert," she warned and moved across the room to scoop him up.

The obedient dog, tail between his legs for the mess he'd caused, didn't move a muscle.

Tessa smiled and dropped the dog on Drake's lap. "Hold him, please."

Only a short look of astonishment graced Drake's face before he turned all attention to adjusting the wiggling puppy to his grip.

"Sam, go get a banana," Tessa said, scooping Sam up, and setting him just inside the kitchen on the perch. She was referring to the fresh banana Kellie had just brought out. Kellie had learned quickly what Sam did and did not like. "Thank you, Kellie."

Turning back Tessa said, "Steaks aren't good for you. The flesh..."

"I know, I know. It has too much fat in it and therefore clogs the arteries causing problems in later years. Tell me, is everyone out in California like you?''

''I'm perfectly sane. It's the people who eat half-dead animals you should question.''

''Half-dead?'' Drake paused in his juggling of the dog and glanced at Tessa in astonishment. ''I don't kill them. I have them slaughtered. But I can guarantee you they are fully dead when I eat them.'' He burst into laughter.

The dog, taking this to mean playtime, started licking Drake.

Traitor, Tessa thought sourly. Drake sitting there holding the dog as he did, grinning at the puppy and the puppy's tail wagging made him look all too vulnerable and likeable. Very likeable, she realized.

To hide that, she concentrated on what he said and turned her nose up at him.

''Have you ever tried meat?'' Drake questioned, finally getting the puppy under his arm and using his left hand to pet him.

''Never,'' Tessa said. She didn't like the gentle conciliatory way Drake stared at her. It didn't make him look obstinate at all, but kind, patient and caring. She'd found out over the last few days he could be that, but he could also be a very determined man. "My parents were strict vegetarians."

"I'll make you a deal," Drake finally offered.

"What's that?" Tessa asked warily. She'd also learned over the last week or so that this man had a way of manipulating her to his own ends. It was that lopsided smile of his, she thought, or maybe the earnest look in his eyes when he started bargaining. How could anyone resist that?

"I'll read these books every Wednesday and Friday and will have my brother take me out when I want meat if you oblige me and find me something else to read the rest of the week."

"That sounds reasonable." Tessa sighed in relief. It sounded very reasonable, she thought. Of course, she knew he wasn't done. He was never done when he started bargaining.

"Now that I've given in," he continued—

and Tessa barely resisted going *Ah ha!*—"I'd like you to give some, too."

Here it came, she thought. "How's that?"

"Why are you a vegetarian?"

Tessa shrugged. "It's my way of life."

"You don't have anything against eating animals?"

She shuddered. "If they're raised, as you insist, for food, I suppose not. I've just never acquired a taste for it."

"Then if you succeed in teaching me like you say you will, I want you to agree, at the end of our lessons, to just try one meal with me. It'll be a healthy meal. I promise."

Tessa's stomach turned. "I'm being paid to teach you. Why should I eat a meal that I don't want?"

"So I'll stop eating it in your house?" he asked mildly.

"We'll see," she muttered.

"Not good enough," he countered.

"Okay, okay. Just no more meat in my house."

He nodded. "Agreed. And better reading material for me?"

She sighed. "I'll try to find you something, Drake. I'm not sure what it'll be, though. I guess teaching an adult is a bit different than working with kids."

Drake grinned his lopsided grin, his eyes glowing with that gentle humor of his. "I hope so."

"So, what do you want to do since it seems the lesson for today is over?"

"Go outside."

Surprised, Tessa sat back and stared while stroking Missy, who had at some point returned to her and curled up in her lap. "You haven't gone outside much this week."

Drake ran a hand through his hair. "I've been too exhausted, if you want the truth."

"Stan has certainly been putting you through a workout."

Tessa lifted the cat from her lap and toed the lizard until it lifted its huge green body and lumbered off. Once standing she moved to get his wheelchair.

"Please," he said, stopping her with his gentle words. "I want the walker. I don't want that thing while I'm here."

"What did Stan say?"

Drake scowled. "Not to tire myself too much. If I take it slow, though, I can make it."

She hesitated. Drake's gaze met hers. "I know, Tessa, you aren't a nurse and you've taken on more than you thought you would, but..."

Compassion filled Tessa's heart. Actually, it hadn't been too bad at all. True, she was doing more than she had thought, but Drake's curiosity and need to talk about God relaxed her, taking off what should have been a heavy burden of having two extra people in her house. And, she had to admit, though Drake could be stubborn as a mule sometimes, he did try not to make more work for her. Feeling the last of the tension drain away she offered him a soft word of encouragement. "Let's do it. It's the only way you'll build muscle."

She was rewarded with a fresh sparkle of encouragement in his eyes.

After going into his room, Tessa returned with the walker. She held on to it and stood where she could help him up. "Your grip is getting stronger," she murmured when the warm long fingers closed and held on tightly. Slowly he pulled himself to a standing position. Tessa watched as he went up and up and finally up. She'd had no idea he was that tall until she'd started helping him.

She came maybe to his nose, she thought. Standing, he seemed so much bigger than the pale, sick invalid in the chair.

Yet he was still the same man.

Gripping the walker, Drake took a breath and slowly released it before testing his balance. "As I said, Stan is working me hard."

"You work yourself hard," Tessa replied. And he did. She could hear him at night when he didn't realize she was awake. He'd get in and out of bed while practicing his words, banging things as he worked on strengthening his muscles.

She was afraid he was doing too much, never letting up. But Stan seemed to think the stamina this man was showing was great.

"What is it with you and Stan?" Drake asked, breaking into her thoughts.

She glanced sideways at him as she strolled alongside him through the living room, into the kitchen and to the back door. "What about him?" Had he read her mind? That was an eerie thought.

She paused to move one of the rabbits back into its cage and then caught up the other one, depositing it where it belonged. She grabbed the toad's cage and carried it outside. She set the cage down before turning to wait for Drake as he reached the top of the shallow ramp.

Slowly, very carefully, they made their way down the ramp and into the grassy yard. Drake sighed and sat down in one of the iron chairs. He was gorgeous, she thought. Those eyes of his were so captivating. How she had enjoyed his company since he'd been here, his friendship, his questions. There wasn't much she didn't enjoy, except his mule stubbornness. She couldn't help but smile.

"Stan comes over here for more than my therapy, Tessa," he murmured now.

She liked the way he'd learned to say her name. His speech was improving daily. In the time he'd been here, his hair had grown out to where just the white line on his head showed. A lot of the pink had been covered now. Still, the scars on his face were bright, something that would take time to go away, she guessed. The white of his skin was not as bad. Getting up and moving had evidently restored circulation. He looked fresher, more alive than he had when he'd arrived. His trips outside with his brother had obviously helped as well.

Tessa checked on her turtles, pausing to make sure the hummingbird feeders were filled and the bird feeders had plenty of water and food. While she did all of this, she debated how to answer Drake.

They had really gotten to know each other in their daily chat sessions. They were more than strangers now, more than polite friends. They had formed some sort of odd bond, she thought. It was there, though neither spoke of it. It was as if talking so much, sharing so many of the same views had given them permission to go a step further and delve into each other's personal lives—a place where casual friends wouldn't go. She also admired him. The way he worked, fought, struggled to overcome his ailments made her sit up and take notice. What had he been like before?

The rumors she heard were not of that. Not at all. They'd described a man who ran his ranch and ran it hard. He was bringing his brother up the same way, she'd heard. He was a womanizer and heavy drinker and liked to go out of the county to party. He was responsible, and his ranch was one of the bigger ranches in the area. She wondered if the rumors had been wrong. Or was it that he had simply and truly changed when he'd asked Jesus into his heart. She knew a life-changing experience like that could change the hardest of people.

"Stan was my therapist for a while. You've seen how it is with therapists. You grow close and friendly." Tessa moved over and sat down in another of the iron rocking chairs.

"Ah," Drake murmured in understanding. "You know my brother asked me about that."

Surprised, Tessa glanced his way. Instead of continuing with that line, he paused to lean over and fumble with his shoes. First one, and then the other came off. Slowly he worked his socks off and then sank his feet into the grass.

"Why would he want to know about that?" she questioned when he didn't say anything else.

Despite what Drake had been through, his movements were smooth as he slowly stretched his legs out. Pleasure slipped over his face. The glow as he ran his feet through the slightly tall, in-need-of-a-cut lawn reminded her of standing out in the fresh spring rain and enjoying the feel of it as it fell gently down on her.

Murmuring a slightly slurred reply, he said, "The way Stan acts. He's very possessive of you."

Tessa sighed, the pleasant picture fading to one of the past. "I know. He has no claim on me. To be honest, Drake, I haven't dated since several years ago, when I lived in California. I think Stan is just interested."

"Are you interested?" The soft query next to her filled with warmth and concern surprised her. How did this man who had so many problems of his own pick up on her worry and zero right in on what was the matter?

"I don't know. Honestly. At one time I thought I'd be, but I've started my life over. I'm not sure I want to go back to the life before…before I changed. I don't think I can. I mean, who needs dating?" She shrugged, not looking at Drake.

The soft touch of a hand brought her gaze around. He smiled at her. "Tell me another story from the Bible."

She chuckled. He had such a way of turning her mind from worrisome subjects. Even in his condition. "You're worse than the kids at school badgering me to tell them a story!"

Drake liked her chuckle, the way her eyes sparkled when she wasn't thinking about the past. For some reason anything to do with men darkened her gaze—men and California, that was. What exactly had happened out there besides an earthquake to put such a haunted look in her eyes? That look was why he'd asked her to tell him a story. She was wonderful when she was in her storyteller mode. The ghosts fled, her eyes lit up. "Consider me a big kid," he said, now watching the slow animation overtake her features.

"But you won't read those books," she argued.

"They're silly," he countered, thinking how simple the books were and how they held nothing of interest for a man of his age.

"Okay, okay, tell me what you want to hear about."

"Pick a parable today," he murmured.

"How about the wise man who built his house upon the rock instead of sand?"

"That's the only place to build a house," Drake replied, wondering what she was talking about. He was only halfway through the Children's Old Testament. Having never read his Bible before, he was finding it fascinating and working to devour every word. That story he hadn't come upon yet, though. "Any sane person knows that."

"It's a parable, remember. It has many meanings."

"Okay, okay. Go on."

"When the rains came, the house built upon the sand was washed away."

Drake nodded. "Like a hurricane hitting the coast?"

"Exactly."

"Jesus was using that parable to talk to us about different things."

"What do you think He meant?" Drake asked, enjoying watching her and listening to her voice.

Today she was again dressed casually. Her long brown hair hung down in corkscrew curls to the middle of her shoulder blades. It was caught back with a strip of soft blue material, with only a few small tendrils escaping its grasp. Her light blue shirt and darker blue fitted pants made the blue of her eyes glow.

He wondered if she had any idea how beautiful she was sitting there. He'd certainly learned all about her zany ways since he'd been here. Her animals, the way she read constantly when she thought he was sleeping. And she liked to sing.

Off-key.

She was certainly a character—sweet and innocent. He didn't know such creatures existed in the here and now—except...

He thought she was hiding something from her past. He wasn't sure what, but underneath that innocent veneer there was something dark that bothered her.

He felt like he'd known this woman his entire life. Right now she was his lifeline to learning again. They'd spent endless hours together trying to make sense of the books she had and the phonics she taught. And it was working. He had to admit that.

"Well, if you go back into the Bible, just before that, Jesus is talking about people bearing fruit and the fact that some are trying to get the splinter out of the other person's eye instead of seeing to the log in their own."

"Two-faced people?" Drake asked.

Tessa leaned forward and toed off her black shoes before running her own toes through the soft cool grass under the huge maple tree. Drake inhaled the fresh scent of the nearby apple blossoms as he waited for her to continue.

"Not really," she finally admitted. "I think He was talking more about people putting on airs. People who were self-righteous. People who insisted on always being right. Setting themselves up in positions of authority and leaders."

Drake nodded. "And?"

"And that these people were so concerned about putting others down or controlling them that they never really looked to the heart of God, what God called us to do."

"To serve Him and love each other."

Tessa nodded. "Exactly. So many want to control other people."

A dark cloud passed in Tessa's eyes as she said that. Drake cocked his head slightly, studying her. "Controlling others isn't our job."

"No. It's not."

"What about being in control?" he asked softly.

Her gaze snapped to his. "Control should be ours."

Drake frowned. "I wasn't in control when that bull decided to do a tap dance on my head."

"Well, yeah," she started.

"God was though, Tessa."

"Well, yeah," she said again.

He'd definitely hit upon an area that she didn't like to discuss. *Control.* Deciding to change his tactic, he commented, "I'm surprised you let me stay in your house. I appreciate it, though."

"I'd rather you be here than have to go somewhere to teach you."

"Ah," he nodded. There was that control factor again. At least, if he looked at it from that point of view it explained many things he'd seen in the house. She had a dozen locks on the doors, followed a strict schedule, had to have everything in a certain place. Anytime something was moved or changed she got flustered and went on and on about the problem. Only her animals were allowed to cause an upset or throw something out of kilter.

"So, God is telling us if we listen to what He says and aren't self-righteous then we'll be like the man who built his house upon the rock?"

She nodded. He could see she was relieved to be back to the subject at hand. "Exactly. As you said, only a hardheaded person, who had no real care for his life, would build his house upon the sand. Our pastor spoke once about something really interesting in this area. He said when we get things out of order and stop depending on God as our provider, then we're building our own house, on our own soil. Since Jesus is the cornerstone—the rock we should be building on—when we're not following the will of God, we're building on that sand, building sandcastles, so to speak."

Drake chuckled. "Sounds like a wise man."

"If you'd like to try it tomorrow, we can go to my church. It's a nice little church a couple of miles from here. They're having a cookout tomorrow, too—which is supposed to be fun. I missed the picnic last month."

"I think I've heard something about the locals going to a picnic every so often at church. Lots of people do that around here."

"I believe you'd enjoy it. And, Drake, if you're as interested in God as you say you are, church is one of the places to learn."

He nodded. Drake felt like a starving man who hadn't eaten in months and suddenly had a feast set before him. He'd gotten a bit carried away asking questions of Tessa, but she seemed to enjoy answering them. Church would of course, be the next logical step.

"I'm not sure...I mean, like this?" he questioned, suddenly unsure about his appearance.

"Oh, Drake," she said. The way she said that, the look she gave him, melted his worry right away. When she reached out and curled her hand around his, he would have done anything in that moment for her. "The parable we just discussed, remember? We're not supposed to judge each other, or worry, for that matter, about how we each look. We're simply supposed to build our house on Him. Don't worry or do what you believe others think or want. I'm sure you'll gather your stares, but then, since you've never been in the church before I'm sure you would anyway. You know most of these people though, and I think you'll be surprised at how welcome they'll make you.''

"So, get in the will of God and get into church with others or start building sandcastles?" he asked, teasing Tessa.

She chuckled, turning pink. He loved to watch the color stain her cheeks like that. "Well, I hadn't meant it like that, but yeah. God tells us not to forsake the assembling together. That's where we learn. That's where we draw strength. That's where we make friendships. We need each other. We need to learn. We need our church."

"Okay. I'll try it if you think they'll accept me."

"Why wouldn't they?" she asked now. "And why would it matter?"

He shifted uneasily. "Tessa. You're new here—basically. I haven't led the life of a saint. I've had my wild days, my bad days

I've done some things people aren't likely to forgive.''

"It's not them you have to worry about disappointing, Drake.''

Her eyes shone with compassion and understanding. Well, so much for that. She'd obviously heard the rumors about him. "I know."

"Then don't worry. God's the only one you have to please. Listen to Him and everything will be okay."

In that moment, Drake realized this woman wasn't half-bad. Not at all. As a matter of fact, he thought, if he wasn't so scarred up and had not had such a checkered past, he just might have considered asking her out when he got better.

"I'd better get back inside and call my brother about tomorrow. See if he wants to come."

"Good idea."

Slowly he stood and with her help tottered back into the house like an eighty-year-old man. At thirty-eight he shouldn't walk this

way. But like Tessa said, he should just thank
God and make the best of it.

And try not to think of what he missed out
on with Tessa Stanridge because of his injuries.

Chapter Seven

"You really didn't have to go with us to church," Tessa murmured to Stan as he moved past Tessa toward a seat on the opposite side of Drake.

"This is an awful long time for him to be out on his own."

"Don't services usually last a half hour or so?" Liam asked, drawing a surprised look from Tessa.

Stan shrugged off the question and took his seat. Liam followed Stan. She took the seat on the other side of Drake, wondering if she should answer Liam's question or not.

But Tessa didn't know about any services he might have attended. The way Drake had talked, neither he nor Liam had ever really been inside a church—at least not since they were old enough to pay attention to what was actually going on. She wondered what Liam would think when he realized these services did last over an hour usually, if she included the time of singing and offering. And then, of course, there were the announcements and people going up for prayer if they were sick.

She wondered if Stan had mentioned it, then decided because of his schedule when he was here in Hill Creek, he may never have made it through an entire service either. He used to visit Hill Creek only for emergencies, he'd told her. Until now. Because he was assigned to Drake, all of that would change. He was in for a pleasant surprise.

"I feel under-dressed," Drake murmured, interrupting her thoughts.

Glancing at Drake in his dark blue jeans and white button-down shirt, she thought he looked so handsome.

"Look over there," she murmured low.

"Sheriff McCade is in khaki pants and a blue shirt similar to yours, and his brother Zach, well, forget Zach. He's the oldest. The oldest always think they have to look the best."

"I'm the oldest," Drake said dryly.

Tessa grinned. "See? What did I tell you? So that means you aren't under-dressed."

"I don't see what dressing up has to do with anything. Pretty hypocritical if you ask me," Liam murmured, his gaze going from one person to another. "Is this supposed to be a meat market where everyone checks everyone else out?"

Tessa sighed. "No, Liam. It's not. That's what I meant. It doesn't really matter what you wear." She squirmed a bit uncomfortably. She hadn't really ever talked to someone so obviously against basic Godly beliefs, so she was finding this conversation with Liam very discomfiting. "It's just well, your heart that matters."

Stan overheard that and chuckled. Elbowing Liam he said, "My heart is perfectly healthy. Just had an EKG the other day."

Liam joined in the chuckle. Tessa wasn't sure if she was pleased or not at Stan's joke.

Drake wasn't, if his frown mirrored what was in his soul. She could see the wheels turning in his mind and held her breath waiting to hear what he might say. It wasn't long in coming. "If you'd be more comfortable waiting outside…"

Stan glanced sharply at Drake. Liam as well reacted negatively. His gaze traveled over Drake before he shook his head. "No problem. I'll stay right here."

"Stan?" Drake asked.

Glancing past Drake to Tessa, Stan winked. "I was only teasing Tessa. I enjoy going to church occasionally." He grinned.

Tessa, feeling an unaccountable rise in tension turned her head to avoid meeting anyone's eyes. She had thought Stan a Christian but with the jokes and comments, she had to wonder. Perhaps he was just nervous. She so wanted this morning to be perfect for Drake. She had been so excited for him. *He* had been so excited.

Seeing friends she smiled, hoping to ease

the high emotions around her. She waved to Mitch's wife. "That's Suzi," she said, referring to the dark-haired Hispanic woman next to the tall, lean sheriff of Hill Creek. "And over there," she continued, pointing to a young woman whose dark blond hair was French-braided against her head, "is Angela, Zach's daughter who is starting her first year of college this fall. The child graduated early with honors in January. She comes over often to check on my pets."

"A pet lover, is she?" Drake murmured low. Relieved to hear his steady, calm voice that revealed no tension at all, she nodded. "Angela is going to be a vet, she said."

While conversing with Drake, Tessa noted the other two had relaxed slightly and fell into a quiet general conversation. Barely cocking her head toward them, she cut her eyes to Drake and smiled. She mouthed, *thank you* and then indicated the other two.

Drake grinned and rolled his eyes. The expression was so comical with the tiny scars along one side of his face pulling as they were that Tessa barely kept from chuckling.

The pastor came to the pulpit and people stood. Music began and then they sang songs. Tessa kept a close eye on Drake, not entirely trusting him to Stan's care—especially with Liam standing right there watching the both of them as well as his brother. He seemed to be waiting for something to happen.

She wondered if she'd been that callous and rude before she'd actually returned to God. Didn't Liam see how much this meant to Drake, how worried he was about his first impression? Couldn't Liam tell how hard it was for him, at his age, to come into the church where most of the people there knew what type of life he'd led before the accident? She had been surprised by Stan's reaction, too. Or maybe Stan had simply been raised in church and wasn't sensitive to the spiritual side of things like he was the physical.

She noted when Drake's curiosity and surreptitious glances changed to determination and sheer fortitude. When Stan leaned over and whispered, she took a guess it was to tell him to sit down.

With a slight shake of his head, Drake returned his attention to the front. He was downright stoic when the pastor told them all to be seated.

She wondered why.

Then she saw the thin line of sweat on his brow and knew she'd been right earlier. He was tired and Stan had noted that.

Realizing that Stan really was keeping a close watch on Drake, Tessa returned her attention to the front. Liam wouldn't have anything to complain about here. According to Drake, Liam didn't want his brother going to church. He'd been certain it was some sort of setup, that they were going to do some weird religious thing like drag him to the front of the church and make him jump up and down and say he wasn't sick.

Tessa was still amused over that. She really thought that was probably why Liam had come—to protect his brother. And she had to admire him for that. Despite his fears, Liam loved his brother.

Could Drake see that? she wondered.

They prayed, and then sang some slower worship songs. She didn't stand this time as only some of the people were on their feet. She wanted to make sure Drake stayed put.

Finally the pastor told the rest of the congregation to be seated and opened his Bible.

She felt Drake relax, his muscles loosening as he settled in to listen. Liam, on the other hand, shifted, causing the pew to creak loudly.

Tessa smiled. Little things like Liam's distrust or the tiny noises wouldn't bother her. She wouldn't let them after finally coming back to God. It'd taken nearly dying for her to realize it didn't matter what other people did, what they said or didn't say. It only mattered what her relationship with God was.

God was faithful by leading her to this wonderful little church, where they had their problems like any other group of people. They worked together, played together and prayed together—in and out of the church. It didn't matter if it was a person's first visit or if that person had been a member forever, the group made sure that person was included.

Amazingly enough, the pastor preached on

forgetting those things which are behind and looking forward to the things before us.

She couldn't have been happier to hear such a message. It was a good thing for Drake to hear, to remind him that the past was the past.

She squirmed a bit though as the message made her think of what she'd let go. *But God, how can I? How can I just forget what happened in the past?* But the pastor continued on with the message reminding all that God was in control, that it was God who we must believe in and trust.

In no time at all they were having the altar call. Liam didn't wait but stood and strode out of the church. Stan glanced up, his surprised gaze on Liam before he cut his eyes to Tessa in query.

Tessa glanced toward where Liam had disappeared and then leaned over toward Drake. ''Drake?''

''I should be with him, I think,'' Drake murmured low. ''He has a lot of past that is haunting him.''

Puzzled, Tessa nodded. ''Let's go.''

Stan nodded and they quietly stood, not disturbing the music or those who had gone forward for prayer, and very slowly and carefully they slipped out the back.

Drake did wonderfully, one slow step at a time. She was amazed at how well he did without the walker or any other type of help. But he'd refused to go to church like that. He'd wanted to go in under his own power.

Liam waited outside, leaning against the handrail, his gaze up on the early afternoon clouds that were spotting the sky.

''I'll go get the car,'' Stan said. He was driving Drake's luxury car that the Slaters drove occasionally if they went on road trips. Liam had seen that it was delivered last night.

Tessa stayed next to Drake who stood, holding on to the rail next to the ramp.

Finally Liam turned, his hands rested on his waist, one leg cocked and a scowl on his face. ''That sounds so easy, doesn't it? What they were saying.''

Drake shook his head. ''No, Liam. Not at all.''

''Sure it does. Just let go of the past and

go on. What do they expect, some fairy to come sprinkle fairy dust and take away the memories?''

Drake lifted a hand helplessly then let it fall.

Tessa, seeing that Drake didn't have an answer, provided her own. "I don't think they mean that at all, Liam. I think what was meant was that you have to learn to live after the pain. Don't dwell on the past but look to what God has for your future.''

Liam snorted.

Stan arrived with the car.

Seeing the car, Liam strode over to it and pulled open the door. "Help my brother. I'll drive.''

Tessa felt Drake stiffen. "Gently,'' she whispered.

"The picnic,'' he suddenly said.

Tessa shook her head. "More important things.'' Louder, she said, "Liam. We were going to stop for a bite to eat on the way back to my house, if you'd like to join us. Is there any reason for you to hurry back out to the ranch?''

Drake glanced at her, his brows raised in astonishment. She simply smiled then mouthed, *he needs you.*

Liam didn't glance her way, staring out the front windshield instead. Finally he nodded shortly. "There's a steak house up the road. Let's go there."

Steak, Tessa thought, weakly. Why did everyone have such a fetish about steak in these parts?

"I'm not sure…" Drake began.

Realizing Drake was about to veto the idea because of Tessa's feelings about meat, she stopped him. Laying a hand on his arm, she interrupted, "That sounds great."

Chapter Eight

The restaurant wasn't crowded though there were quite a few people. Many waved to Liam and just as many avoided looking directly at Drake.

Stan helped Drake into a seat and then sat across from him. Tessa and Liam took seats across from each other. Drake didn't mind where Tessa was seated since it was close enough so that he could talk to her. He'd found that he enjoyed and even looked forward to her company.

Studying his brother as the waitress brought the menus, Drake decided to say nothing about church but to dive into other things that were bothering him. He felt a responsibility for his brother and what he was going through right now, in more areas than one. "What did the doc say about the cows?"

Drake opened his menu and pretended to be reading it though he already knew what he wanted.

Out of his peripheral vision he saw his brother start at his actions then glance at Tessa before back at him. "Diseased. We're gonna have to kill an eighth of our herd."

Drake sighed. "That's going to cost us a lot."

"I've been going over the books. I'll see everything is okay, Drake."

Drake didn't argue.

The waitress took their orders.

"Just salad for me," Tessa said politely smiling.

Drake couldn't help but be distracted by her words. "You sure you don't want to share a steak with me, Tessa?" he drawled.

He ignored the other two men's curious gazes and continued to prod Tessa.

Her nose went up, her cheeks flushed bright. "No. I think not. Especially if they're now diseased."

He chuckled.

"I'll have steak and potato, too," Stan murmured. "And an explanation about that last comment, if you will, Tessa?"

Drake chuckled. "We have an agreement going. Sooner or later she is going to have a steak dinner with me."

Stan chuckled.

Liam simply glanced from one to the other, confused.

Drake grinned. "I didn't tell him."

"Tell me what?" Liam asked.

"You didn't tell him?" Tessa demanded of him. Her eyes sparked with emotion and she glared at him.

"He doesn't know about Tessa?" Stan asked, amusement lacing his voice.

Liam looked downright alarmed now. "What's going on?"

Drake shrugged. He found himself actually enjoying his brother's discomfiture. It took his mind off his condition, got his mind off the worries of the ranch. Resisting a smile, he said, as if it were something he wouldn't be caught dead saying, "I'm not telling him. Go ahead, Tessa."

He turned his attention to the tea glass the waitress set in front of him. Grabbing up the sugar with his left hand, he placed it in his right and worked to tear open the sugar and dump it in the glass without spilling.

"What is it, Miss Stanridge?" Liam asked, his attention off Drake and now on Tessa. Relieved, Drake finished the preparation of his tea and allowed his smirk to show.

Tessa kicked Drake under the table.

He jumped, dropping his spoon. His gaze shot to her.

She promptly blushed red.

Drake muffled his laugh, knowing the other two had no idea why she was turning such a shade of red.

"Call me Tessa," she muttered and grabbed her own herbal tea to take a sip.

Liam looked from Stan, who was grinning from ear to ear, back to Drake. "Drake? I don't appreciate being kept in the dark. Especially if this has something to do with you—"

"She doesn't eat meat." Drake just dropped the statement out into the middle of the table, interrupting his brother, with no explanation at all. One simple sentence. He knew, however, it would again distract his brother from his "condition" and push certain buttons Liam had. He waited with pleasure, watching Tessa as she glared at him with an *I'm going to get you* look.

"I mean if…" Liam paused. "Huh?"

Drake carefully picked up his glass, making sure his hand was steady, and took a sip. Then he set it back down. Turning to meet his brother's stunned gaze he nodded, waiting just the appropriate amount of time before reiterating, "She doesn't eat meat."

"You mean like, chicken and cows and things?" Liam asked, disbelief rife in his escalating voice.

"Not everyone does, Liam," Tessa replied. "And yes, I do believe those are the correct type of *things* that give us meat."

Drake glanced over at Tessa's remark. She

looked so prim and proper sitting there, her nose in the air, holding her herbal tea, eyebrows raised as if instructing a bad student.

Stan resisted chuckling as he accepted his salad from the waitress. But Liam continued to stare at Tessa. His gaze went from stunned disbelief to close observation, like Tessa might be from another solar system instead of good old planet Earth where meat—at least in these parts—was the number one source of all vitamins, minerals, vegetables and whatever else a body might need.

Drake thoroughly enjoyed watching his brother unable to bowl over a woman with only a look. Every time Liam and Tessa were in the same room, Liam ended up with just such a look on his face.

"Buck up, little brother. It's not the end of the world."

"But we *sell* cattle for consumption," he argued.

"Not to her you don't," Stan murmured and took a bite of his salad.

"Not to her," Drake agreed.

Liam looked back at her. Tessa shrugged. "Not to me."

Liam muttered something under his breath and stabbed at his salad. He then stared at it as if it had done something awful to him and shoved it aside in disgust.

Tessa lifted her gaze to meet Drake's.

He grinned.

A reluctant smile curved her lips, her eyes going soft as they met his humor-filled ones. Drake loved that look.

"So, how are you coming on lifting the fork and spoon as well as cutting?" Liam asked Drake.

A heaviness descended on Drake. Twice he'd tried to distract his baby brother. Twice Liam had shown Slater stubbornness by returning to the subject despite the warning look Drake gave him.

Deciding not to make a scene because they were in public and because he was already tiring, he looked down at his silverware. "I'm doing better."

What could he tell his brother? Anything negative at all would worry him.

"Did they find out what disease the cows had?" Tessa broke in, changing the subject back.

Drake glanced at her wondering if she realized just what a relief the conversation was. He didn't like talking about his health with his little brother.

At least, he was glad until Liam said just what was the matter with the cattle. "We're going to have an epidemic on our hands," Drake said low, shock reverberating through him at Liam's announcement.

Liam sighed. "Yeah."

"Is the vet out checking other herds?"

Liam nodded wearily. "He thinks the McCade ranch might have a few. He's on his way out there tomorrow for testing. Zach evidently called him last night but he's backed up until tomorrow."

"This isn't good," Drake muttered and then carefully lifted his fork. While eating with Tessa, he had noticed more and more that he'd gotten to where he could lift his fork and even cut some. Cutting was still hard. It was slow, but he managed. Just not like a thirty-eight year-old man should be able to do.

"No. We've been lucky these past few years with no problems. I sure hope this disease hasn't spread through the entire area."

Tessa interrupted. "What disease?"

Drake glanced her way. "A mutated form of brucellosis, which makes cows very sick. Nursing mothers can infect the babies and you can lose an entire herd for the year. Worse, it's contagious, so if you don't get it under control soon it can wipe out an entire herd. Bangs disease or brucellosis causes cattle to spontaneously abort."

Drake wiped a hand down his face. "It doesn't necessarily cause all cows to lose their babies, but it is passed through the diminished milk supply and will cause sterility in other cows. It's so new that most of us still don't know the long-range effects."

"Oh, no," Tessa said, sobering. She'd never heard of anything like that.

"Veterinary medicine has made giant leaps, however," Liam said. "Immunizations and such."

"I only thought you had to worry about cooking them wrong...."

Drake reached out and touched her hand. "That's the least of the worry. If you make sure they're okay before, then cooking isn't as big of a problem as it was years ago."

Their steaks and her special salad came, and Tessa said the prayer before they began to eat.

She didn't say a word when Stan reached over to help Drake cut his food or show him a trick or two. Instead, she addressed Liam. "You know, as long as I've lived out here, I've never been out to a ranch where there are cattle. I suppose many of my assumptions are skewed."

"You should come out sometime then and meet our herd. You might find they aren't as bad as you think." He offered her a friendly smile.

"You shouldn't really be out around them, Tessa," Stan broke in. "It might be too dangerous, especially for you."

Tessa's gaze shot to Stan's. As if realizing

he might have broken confidentiality he had the grace to redden.

Drake's gaze lifted from his attempts to cut his meat to Stan's. "Why?" Then he glanced at Tessa. "Is there something…"

Glancing down at her salad she tried to decide how much to tell him.

"I'm sorry, Tessa. Perhaps we should change the subject." Stan at least offered her a way out.

"No. Really, it's fine." Looking up she met each man's eyes. "I used to live in California. I was out there a few years ago when that seven-point earthquake hit. The building I was in at the time collapsed. It was an older high-rise and not quite up to standards. Actually that's how I ended up giving my heart back to my God."

She thought that an understatement. She wasn't going to go into details so she simply added, "I ended up having to have my own therapy for nerve damage in my left leg."

"Oh, well, then that explains how you know Stan. Therapy. You had said that, but we wondered if something had happened here or…''

She tuned out Liam's words as she met Drake's eyes. In his eyes were curiosity and something else. His gaze probed her, searching, seeking answers to unasked questions. It was like he knew that was only a pebble in a quarry full of explanations of what had happened to her.

But he wouldn't pry—at least not now. Instead he nodded.

Glancing around, she realized both Stan and Liam stared at her expectantly. ''Drake should be getting home and so should I. I have many pets that are going to be wondering why they haven't been fed yet,'' she said.

Tessa glanced down at Drake's meal and saw he'd eaten well over half of it. ''You're doing better.''

He nodded. ''I'm doing better.''

Liam cleared his throat. ''So now that you've been to church, Drake, I suppose you won't be going anymore?''

Tessa wondered how he'd managed to stay off the subject so long. But he had. Until now.

She sat back quietly and let Drake and his brother have the floor.

"No, Liam, I will go. I enjoyed the service and it filled an empty spot that sorely needed filling."

Tessa ached. Reaching out, she slipped her hand over his hand that lay on the table. Instantly his fingers curled around her hand, gripping it. Their eyes met and something indefinable passed between them.

Helping him stand, she continued to stare. He hesitated only a moment before he reached out and hugged her. "Thank you," he murmured.

She wrapped her arms around him, not sure what he was thanking her for, maybe just for listening or being there. But whatever it was, she found she certainly liked being in his arms. Still, she knew it couldn't last. Pulling back, she whispered, "You're welcome. Anytime."

With those words, they slowly made their way to the door where Stan had the car waiting. Before they got in, however, Drake leaned over and said softly, "I have a small request."

Tessa paused, glancing at Drake who was half-in, half-out of the car. "What's that?"

"I want you to tell me someday what really happened in California and what drove you back to God."

Chapter Nine

The animals were fed. The guests gone. Kellie had gone into her room for an afternoon nap.

It was simply Drake and Tessa in the living room. Even her cat and dog were snoozing.

"How are you feeling?" she asked Drake, going over and sitting down in a chair next to the sofa where he sat.

"Tired," he murmured slowly.

He looked tired. "I have a surprise for you," she whispered.

Lifting tired eyelids, he smiled at her. That smile could melt butter on a winter day, she thought. Despite the scars, or maybe because of the scars, he had the ability to smile like that, his eyes full of…interest? Was that what she saw?

"What?" she asked.

"I'm just thinking I might like a surprise from you," he whispered right back.

Heat stole into Tessa's cheeks. "I think I'm finally seeing the real you, Drake Slater," she said and stood. Going over to her desk, she pulled out an envelope. After returning to his side, she dropped it in his lap. "Open it," she said, ignoring the continued chuckle at her remark.

Reseating herself, she waited.

Drake shifted the large envelope to where he could work the top part loose. Turning it upside down he shook it. Five different sheets of paper fell into his lap.

Glancing up in surprise, he asked, "What's this?"

She blushed a bit darker, embarrassed now that she had to confess to what she'd been up to so many nights lately. "Stories."

Puzzled, he glanced back down at his lap

and shuffled through them, separating them and picking one up. "Typed pages."

"I typed them. You'll notice the print is a bit bigger than normal type—that's what a good computer can do for you."

"You have pictures of…cattle in here?"

"And other things," she defended. "I found pictures online and different clip art sites. The book you are holding right there is about God owning the cattle on a thousand hills. You'll see the scripture references."

"And the others?" he asked, moving the first one aside to scan through the next ones.

Clasping her hands, she shrugged. She stood and moved closer to where she could see which ones he picked up. "Ah, well, that one there, with the pictures of the Ark of the Covenant is about the calling of Samuel. The one with the sling and stones is…"

"About David? I've read a bit of that."

"Yes." More encouraged she moved on to the next one. "This is a New Testament story as well as this one. But you'll have to read them and tell me what they're about."

She grinned cheekily.

He chuckled. "Ever the teacher."

Nodding, she agreed. When he reached out and cupped her cheek, however, she forgot this was a teaching lesson or that she was a teacher. All she was aware of was that this was a very kind, gentle and caring man. And she was a woman who had not met anyone like that in a long time.

How she wanted to explore that more...

The squawking of the parrot in the other room caused her to sit back.

"We can put off today's lesson for a while if you want."

"Why, Tessa?" Drake asked, his gaze traveling over her with curiosity and concern.

"You're tired," she replied.

"I am that. But..."

She waited. "But what?"

"I'm glad you'll put off the lesson a while because I'm still waiting to hear a story on California."

Oh well, she could have hoped he'd forgotten. It looked like he hadn't, though. However, if it was the choice of being back in contact with him or telling him that story, she chose the latter, out of pure self-defense.

"You know, Tessa, you don't have to share if you don't want to, but in the last weeks, if nothing else, I feel we've become friends."

Tessa agreed with that. She had developed such an odd bond with Drake. But it was more than friendship, she feared. He was able to capture and hold her attention with just one look from those deep green eyes of his.

"I did tell the truth earlier," she said, now sinking into the comfort of the sofa.

Drake stretched out his legs before shifting the homemade books on his lap. "I know you did, Tess..."

He trailed off.

"But?" she asked.

He nodded. "But."

She sighed.

The only sound in the quiet room was the ticking from the wall clock over the hearth. It echoed loudly as second after second passed. Drake interrupted the silence.

"I've never been in an earthquake," Drake said softly.

Tessa trembled. "It's something you'd never forget."

"I've seen pictures on TV of the deva-station they do. I saw the one you were in a few years ago on TV as well."

Tessa nodded. "It made all of the news. Though it wasn't the 'great' earthquake it was considered a 'major' earthquake. We take for granted the small ones that let off the tension. It'd been a long time since anything had happened to this fault line, though, and one day it simply...went."

Tessa clasped her hands together nervously. She was surprised when Drake's large one fell gently on top of her clasped ones.

She didn't object.

"Have you ever told anyone about this, Tess?"

Twisting her hands slightly she allowed his own hand to open and then wrapped both of her hands around his bigger hand. His skin was getting darker every day from the sun. He loved the outdoors, she realized, reveled in the feel of the heat on his face and hands.

"No," she whispered softly. "I haven't really talked about the past...not really."

"Maybe it might help."

His nails were short, clean, working nails she would call them. Dark hair sprinkled the back of his hand. "I didn't know anyone realized my past bothered me. I'm sorry, Drake, if I haven't been as professional as I should—"

"It's not that at all," he interrupted. Stroking her hand with his thumb, he said, "I've been around long enough to know what pain looks like. In a person's eyes. When we were sitting in church today and we were listening to the pastor, I had to think that just maybe that was your problem as well as mine—the past."

She chuckled. It wasn't a chuckle of amusement but nervousness. "I still have nightmares, you know. Of being trapped..."

"Care to share?"

Tessa shuddered. She wasn't sure why his encouraging voice so easily invited her to share her secrets but it did. Just like his eyes had captured her that first day, his voice captured her now, weaving its spell of safety and confidence around her.

She hadn't had anyone to talk to like this in a long while, not someone that made her feel safe, like she could lean on them. No one, that was, except God. True, she had Leah and Freckles but they were different. With this man she actually felt…safe.

"I was running an errand. For my work. I had stopped by to see Michael on the way back. Michael was my boyfriend at the time—well, actually, fiancé."

"Did he die in the…?" Drake ventured.

Shaking her head, she reassured him. "No. He wasn't in the building. Had he been in his office he most likely would have died. The building collapsed. Over eighty percent of the people in that building, they said, lost their lives that day. It's funny how human lives can be boiled down to statistics. Not numbers like one hundred and forty people, or lists like all but one worker from Prise Corporation, but simple percentages."

"I think that may be how medical people

and emergency workers keep their distance from the horror,'' Drake surmised.

Realizing she was gripping his hand, she eased her hold. She was grateful when he tightened his hold on her hands.

"I'm sure it is. They would have to do something to keep sane after seeing so much death.'' Taking a deep breath, she let it out slowly. "The first sign something was the matter was the building shaking. Then we heard it…the grating sound that accompanies something like that. Except this was worse than any I'd been in before. Never had I felt a building shudder like that.''

Swallowing, she whispered, "Things started flying, the ceiling and insulation of the floor I was on started dropping around us. People screamed. We all ran for spots in the doorway or under something.

"The lights went out.

"It was pitch black and I couldn't see where to go. A loud explosion sounded. Glass breaking. I dove under the nearest desk.''

Tessa swallowed several times. Through a dry throat she whispered, "I was in a free fall. I remember thinking of the astronauts and wondering if that's what they felt like in the space shuttle. And then the pain. I'd never felt pain like that. It was quick and then I didn't remember anything.''

Drake continued to rub her hands with his thumb, slowly, steadily. She was certain that action was somehow providing the strength she needed to go on.

''How did they find you?''

''Dogs.''

''Were you there very...long?'' he asked hesitantly.

She heard the note in his voice and lifted her tormented gaze to his concerned and caring one. ''Two days, Drake, though it seemed like two years. I remember waking up. The pain was awful. I thought I'd lost my legs. A major beam had fallen across my hips. I was in and out of consciousness. I heard no one around me. I knew they were all dead.

''I wasn't, though. And I remember at that moment wishing I was. The pain, you see...''

He squeezed her hands again. They were icy, bloodless as she gripped him.

"But I kept thinking about Michael. I had to live. Michael would blame himself, you see. I was in his building. He wasn't there but I was. If I died, he'd never forgive himself."

"What happened?" Drake asked.

She felt the tears in her eyes and wanted to reach up and wipe them away. Her voice changed to flat and toneless. She didn't want to remember what was next. "I suppose you guessed it must not have been happily ever after with Michael and me?"

"I'm sorry." With a strong, firm squeeze of her hands he continued, "Sometimes things just don't work out, Tessa."

"They rescued me. The dogs found me. I was so hot, so thirsty. I remember pain when they got me out. When I woke up a few days later it was to find out I'd required emergency surgery."

"Was Michael there?"

"Yes, for a while. He was the one who...he wouldn't look me in the eyes when he told me. I had always wanted children, but...I nearly died and was damaged internally."

"I'm sorry, Tess," Drake murmured. Releasing her hands he slipped his arm around her and pressed her shoulders, giving comfort. "That led you back to God then?"

She shook her head. Leaning into his strength she accepted the hug. How very odd it was to feel a man's arm around her. It had been so very long. It was almost alien in nature—and yet welcome. The gentle strength in Drake's hand as he clasped her shoulder, the way his warmth radiated to her, the caring tone in his voice. It was much too much like an addictive drug.

Pulling away, she got up and crossed to get a tissue. Returning, she sat by him and turned to where she could face him. Dabbing at her eyes she said, "Actually, Drake, I knew at that point that God had spared my life for a reason. I didn't understand why because I wasn't serving Him. I was in rebellion after my mother's death. So it just didn't make sense."

Blowing her nose, she set the tissue aside and grabbed another one. Twisting it around her fingers, she said, "Michael avoided coming to visit me after the third day I was conscious. At first I thought it was because of the disaster and all of the work. But as days passed and more and more time went by, as he didn't return my calls, I started to realize that Michael wasn't dealing with my condition any better than I was.''

"He should have been there for you," Drake said simply.

"Maybe it was the shock of my injuries," Tessa allowed. "He finally showed up and told me he needed time. He thought it would be best to allow me to heal and then maybe later we could talk.''

"He deserted you?''

Tessa didn't answer that question. She didn't want to go down that path. She had never told anyone and didn't plan to start now. Instead, she said, "In a way it was a blessing, Drake, that he dedicated himself to his work. Because I was alone while I recovered, I had time to realize how much God meant to me, how much He loved me, how much I needed Him. One night shortly after getting out of the hospital, I rededicated my life to the Lord.''

Drake smiled. ''That's a beautiful story. However…''

His gaze traveled over her. ''Your leg still gives you trouble?''

She patted her left leg. ''Only when I pull the muscles wrong or fall. I don't fall often. But when I was moving in here…'' She lifted her hands helplessly and smiled, glad to be back under control and have that part of the story over with. It hadn't been as bad as she'd feared, telling this man part of her story.

''You fell?'' he asked.

She nodded. ''I limped around in pain for two weeks before it got so bad the principal told me to get it cleared up before school started. That's where Stan comes in.''

Drake nodded. ''And because of your medical problems, you won't date Stan?'' he asked.

Well, he had certainly shocked her with that question. Tessa was certain her jaw had just hit the floor. Shaking her head she forced her mouth closed. "I, uh, uh…" What could she say?

"It's obvious he's interested in you. This entire week he's made sure he had plenty of time with you after my sessions, or hadn't you noticed?"

Tessa stared at him. Why in the world would he notice how Stan felt? And why would he care?

"Even at lunch today he didn't take his gaze off you."

"I just never really considered him that way," she murmured now, strangely disconnected. Was Drake pushing her at this other man, she wondered? Was it possible he had picked up on the fact that she found Stan fascinating and was trying to find a gentle way to push her away? She thought she'd been so careful and had not given any signals at all.

"It might do you good to get out and date," he observed.

Getting perturbed now, she added, "Yeah, it might." What was it with this man? Each time she thought she had him figured out he turned quarrelsome on her or demanding or...or something she wasn't expecting! Exasperated, she glared at him.

The mood in the room changed, she noted. He was no longer smiling. Nor was the warmth there in his eyes. "It might do you good, Tessa, to get out some. I know with me here it's been hard. It's also probably been hard with that jerk deserting you like he did in California. But just because you can't have kids, isn't any reason to hide out. Just some friendly advice," he added.

Well, she thought, simply staring. So much for her feelings for this man. He obviously didn't return them. The gentle feelings and tenderness she'd just experienced faded away to be replaced with confusion and a need to prove herself. "You know," she said, standing, "I think you're right. Stan asked me if I could step out sometime this week for dinner. Maybe I should just go on and take him up on it—if you think you'd be okay here alone with just Kellie?"

Something indefinable flashed in his eyes. "Kellie and I are old friends. We'll be fine," he said.

Abruptly he frowned and pushed himself to his feet. "I'm tired. I think I'd better lay down."

She could only nod. What had gotten into him?

He started slowly across the room. At the hall he paused. Turning, he smiled at Tessa. "Thank you for telling me your story, Tess. God still does perform miracles, doesn't He?"

"Uh, um, yeah."

Without another word he turned and carefully and slowly made his way into his room.

Tessa waited until she heard the door close before she dropped back down to the sofa. "Men!" she said, exasperated. "They're all useless."

Then, in a fit of irritation, she jerked up the phone and dialed Stan's number.

Chapter Ten

"**I** can't believe you're going out!"

Tessa sighed and shoved her hands in the pockets of her pants. "It's not that unbelievable, Freckles."

Freckles giggled. "Come on, come on, get dressed while we talk."

Tessa obeyed. She went over to her closet and pulled out the outfit she planned to wear. "It's not like I've never been out on a date."

"Just with my brother-in-law," Freckles quipped referring to her very short date with Mitch when he was running from his destiny.

Tessa groaned. Slipping off her stretchy

pants and top, she then pulled on a soft cashmere skirt with a loose matching blue top. Shoving the sleeves up to her elbows, she moved over to the table and sat down to throw on some makeup. "Please don't remind me. I'm still not sure why I let Suzi talk me into that. Glad she doesn't hold hard feelings."

Freckles dropped down onto the edge of the bed. "Suzi's a gem. I like having her as a sister-in-law. She's so quiet and gentle— except with Mitch." Freckles giggled. "So, tell me why you finally decided to take Stan up on his offer."

Tessa shrugged, then wiped off the blusher that had ended up in the wrong place because of her actions. "Really, it's no big deal. I'm over the pain and recuperation process I had to go through physically and emotionally. Things are looking up. I'm going to have enough money soon to finish paying off my bills. And it looks like Hill Creek will finally become my official home. Why not go out? Besides *he* doesn't need me here. He even encouraged me to go out."

Freckles eyes widened with confusion before dawning awareness settled. "He told you to go out with Stan? Mr. I've-dated-every-woman-in-the-county Slater?"

"Gee thanks, Freckles. And you suggested *my* house for him to stay at with a reputation like that?"

Freckles airily waved a hand. "He's a Christian now. He needed other Christians to talk to. Besides…"

When Freckles trailed off, Tessa met her gaze in the mirror. What she saw reflected made her gape. "You set us up! You sent him here purposely because…"

"Now, now, Tessa," Freckles said. Standing, she grabbed the brush and started to work on Tessa's hair. "You two would be perfect for each other. You were hurting, hiding in a shell and wouldn't come out for anyone. He needs someone to care and to talk with and I know you love to share about God…and you need someone to talk to. Can I help it if you two might find common interests?"

Tessa scowled. After finishing her makeup she set down the powder and said, "Well, we didn't. This date was his idea. And he's right. I should get out. I've been too cooped up in here lately. I need to get out and see a bit more of life.''

Freckles grinned. "I'm sure you'll see more of life, but don't you see?"

"See what?" Tessa took the brush from Freckles and finished her hair before tying it back with a ribbon.

"It sounds to me like Drake is pushing you away. Which can only mean he is interested in you."

Tessa glanced up sharply. "Don't be silly."

Freckles patted her tummy. "I'm a married woman expecting a baby. I know these things." With a chuckle she dropped down next to Tessa. "Think about it, honey. I have nearly an entire baseball team of brothers and sisters so I know a little about emotions. He is still recovering and adjusting to life. Do you really think with the condition he is in, he is going to dream he has a chance with you? I mean look at him. He looks like... well..."

"He looks fine," Tessa argued.

"Oh, my," Freckles whispered. She reached out and patted Tessa's hand. Smiling, she stood. "I'll tell you what, sweetie, you might want to reconsider going out tonight. This date with Stan is going to bomb."

Freckles moved over to peek out the window.

"No, it won't. I like Stan. He's a nice guy."

Freckles grinned at something and then let the lacy curtain drop. "He won't ring your bell like someone else, I would wager."

"Ring my...wager? That's it. I'm going to find Hawk and tell him his wife has lost all common sense since conceiving."

Freckles's laugh echoed in the small room. Joy made her face shine and her whole complexion glow. "Ah, well, I'm sure Hawk would agree. He's become quite mellow in the last year or so when it comes to me." Grinning cheekily she added, "Besides, I'm sure you wouldn't dare repeat that to another man."

Exasperated that Freckles was right, she

snapped her eye shadow container closed with a loud snap to show her perturbed feelings that her bluff had been called. "Be that as it may, my heart—and my bell—are perfectly safe and unringable by anyone around here. I'm not looking for a soul mate, someone to tie my heart to, I'm simply going out on a date."

"You're right about that," Freckles said backing down. "Go out on a date and enjoy yourself. By the way, you look beautiful. So why don't you go get 'em."

"I will," she agreed.

"Good." Freckles nodded.

Before she could lose her nerve, Tessa left the room and strode to the living room where her date was waiting.

Chapter Eleven

"So he comes in to treat you and walks off with the prize?"

Drake glanced up from the pad in his lap where he worked on his writing skills. "What's that supposed to mean?" Drake growled, though he knew very well what his brother meant.

"Tessa," Liam said. Strolling away from the window after watching Stan leave, he then eased into the chair near his brother.

"What about her?"

Liam chuckled. "Hasn't it been obvious to you? Stan is interested in the woman."

Drake shrugged. "Doesn't matter to me."

"Oh?" Liam rested his left ankle on his right leg. Drake watched the position, knowing it was one of smug satisfaction. "It's me, big brother. I know that look in your eye."

Drake scowled.

Liam sobered. "So, it is true. You are interested in her."

"I don't remember discussing my private life with you," Drake said coolly. He was still upset over watching Tessa and Stan walk out that door with a "be back in a few hours" remark.

"Maybe not, Drake, but I don't want to see you getting hurt."

Drake drew on patience. He had to or he'd say something that his brother didn't deserve right now. He had to remember that Liam was still the younger one and had just the right knack to get under his skin with his words. It was an older brother thing and just because Drake was in recovery and Liam was working the ranch didn't mean that had changed one bit.

"I find Tessa interesting," Drake said slowly.

Liam nodded. "It's obvious. If she weren't so religious…"

Drake took a breath. Then he rubbed a hand down his face. Praying quietly he asked God for wisdom on how to handle this.

"Liam. Because of God I'm alive today. You will never know how wrong I was about my former beliefs."

"Why, Drake?" Liam asked. Dropping his foot to rest on the floor he leaned forward, allowing his hands to dangle loosely between his knees. "Why is God so all-fired important to you suddenly? I know you almost died. But this week…watching you since you've been out of the hospital I have to agree you are making leaps in your recovery…. So why must you get superstitious and religious on us?"

Drake shook his head. "You don't understand, Liam."

"I've heard all the stuff," Liam said shortly. "We used to laugh about the different folks who got drunk on Saturday night and then went to church on Sunday. We'd laugh at their pious actions when they'd say you have to pray, read your Bible, and give your life to God if one of their churchy friends were around.''

Drake knew Liam was right. They had laughed many times at some of the hypocritical people. But now... "I want to tell you something, Liam. Will you listen?"

"As long as you aren't going to start that stuff with me,'' he warned.

Drake saw the spark of irritation in his brother's eyes. He nodded. "I'm not going to say that at all. I want to tell you what has been going on inside me the past few months."

Liam studied Drake warily. "I know what's been going on, Drake. You've only been in the hospital a short time...."

"I mean before the hospital. Over the last year, Liam."

Drake laid his pen and pad aside. Shifting, he began, "Over the last year I started wondering if this is all there was to life. Going out, getting drunk, chasing women, then recovering from the hangover or from a just plain tired feeling and then running the ranch for another week. Week after week, month after month, year after year. I'll tell you something. I was flipping through the channels and heard one of those preachers on TV. I started to flip on by, but he said something that caught my attention. He quoted, almost exactly what I had been feeling, about if there is more out there.''

''You've been listening to those people on TV?'' Liam's eyes widened in disgust.

''No, Liam. Just this one I did. Only because he caught my attention. I was searching for the news show...anyway, I couldn't even tell you which one it was now. But it dug deep down in me. I got to where that's all I could think about night and day, day and night.''

Liam shifted, his gaze darting away from his brother's. ''Drake, I thought it was Sherry over in the next county that had you so preoccupied. I mean—you've never believed in any of this stuff!''

''I know, Liam. Believe me, I know. And

despite hearing that, I wasn't sure if I believed or not. I had heard stories about how *Jesus died for you,* or how *all have sinned and you have to ask Him into your heart.*"

Liam snorted.

Drake agreed. "Yeah. It sounded pretty wild to me too. I mean...some guy who is supposed to be God in the flesh came to earth to die for me? Why? I kept asking that question. Why? And yeah I wasn't perfect. I knew that, but why would some God care so much about that? No one is perfect. Big deal. And what's the big deal about asking Him into your heart?"

Curiously, Liam studied Drake. "I thought you said you liked that stuff now?"

Drake chuckled. "Just listen." Running a hand through his hair, he continued. "These were the questions going through my mind, Liam. The day the bull did a tap dance on me...."

"Yeah?" Liam asked when he paused.

"I had just been asking God if He was real and what all of that really meant."

Liam stared at him.

Drake took a deep breath. Missy came into the room and hopped up onto his lap. Drake rubbed a hand down the sleek fur as he continued, "I'm not sure if it was a vision, a dream or what...but..." Drake glanced down at the cat. Taking a deep breath he whispered, "When I fell I knew it was over. There was no way to escape the bull. I saw twelve hundred pounds of raw savagery coming right at me. I threw up my hands to block him, like that would help at all. But I was caught in that barbed wire, remember. And...well, anyway, I was saved, I think."

Liam didn't move a muscle. He didn't blink. It even looked as if he'd stopped breathing.

"Well?"

Liam opened his mouth—then closed it. Then he opened it again. Finally he said, "What do you mean?"

Drake breathed a sigh of relief. At least his brother hadn't turned his experience down flat. "That bull was headed right towards me and it stumbled. I'm alive. I don't know how it happened. Liam, it made me realize God

answered prayers. He is real. I also realized
He cared about me. Not me in general as a
person on the earth that would procreate one
day and die, but me as an individual. He knew
me. He had cared enough to keep me from
getting killed. And if that was the case, could
He really have sent His son to earth to die for
me?''

Liam shook his head. He glanced away.
Nervously he rubbed his hands on his jeans.

Drake started to shift his feet but realized
Hubert at some point had toddled in and now
lay asleep on them. Looking back at his
brother, he continued. ''Think about it, Liam.
Can you imagine giving up a child for someone you didn't know? I realized how wrong
I was about so many things. It made me see
myself as me, the sinner, the weak man. It
was such a startling revelation, Liam. I
felt…ashamed.''

''Aw…Drake,'' Liam started shifting really uncomfortably now.

''Just listen,'' Drake said. ''Then this
peace came. I'm not sure when it came or if
I was awake, if it was after the surgery or

before the surgery or what. But I realized that the creator of the universe really cared about me, just me. I asked Jesus...not in specific words, but with a simple, 'I accept the truth and I need You.' I drifted in peace after that."

Liam let out a short breath and stood. He strode across the room and jerked back the curtain. "I don't understand how a God who would do that would let *this* happen to you!"

"If He hadn't, Liam, I would still be refusing to believe the truth. I guess God had to incapacitate me to get my attention."

Liam leaned forward to look out the window. He nearly jumped out of his skin when Sam poked his beak in his ear. "It's only Sam," Drake said.

The bird started whistling the "1812 Overture."

Liam glared and strode back across the room. When he dropped into his seat, though, a hiss warned him a Gila monster occupied it.

"I swear, Drake. Not only have you gone crazy but this entire house has!"

Drake didn't bite back at Liam. He imagined Liam was having a really hard time accepting what he'd just told him. Liam moved over to the sofa and took a seat.

Hubert saw the new set of feet, stood, walked the two steps to Liam and dropped on his feet before promptly closing his eyes and going right back to sleep.

Liam sighed miserably. "I came over here in a halfway decent mood."

Drake felt sorry for his little brother. "I know you did, Liam. And I'm glad you came by. I...well I know you've been having a really hard time with everything. That's one reason I thought I should tell you what had really happened to me and why the change."

Liam studied his brother, but instead of wariness there was a weary acceptance in his eyes. "You really are changed?"

Drake nodded.

"I don't understand, Drake," Liam whispered.

In that instance, Drake realized something about his brother. Something that he had never realized before. "You're not going to lose me, Liam. And I'm not here to judge you. You know what my own life has been like. I'm the last one to judge anyone."

Liam looked up at him. But it wasn't the thirty-two-year-old man that looked at him. Instead it was a twelve-year-old boy when he'd burned down a line shack and just knew he was going to be shipped off to a boys' school for what he'd done. "I don't want to...aw..." Liam cursed. "I don't want to lose you," he said.

Drake said softly. "Blood is thick, brother."

Liam nodded.

"Think about what I've said?" Drake asked.

A crooked grin split Liam's face. "How can I not?"

Drake chuckled. "Now can you tell me when they think they'll have this disease problem with the cattle under control?"

Liam shook his head. "No idea. A week, two, maybe three. At least they know what's going on now."

Drake nodded. "I want to know. Don't

hide it from me," he warned. "I want to know if we're going to have any herd to ship this season."

Liam hesitated then nodded. "Okay, big bro." Standing he toed the dog off his boot and then moved over to slap his brother on the back. "I have to go. Have fun waiting up for Tessa."

Laying the cat aside, Drake stood and followed his brother to the door. "Yeah," he murmured and watched his brother leave.

Tessa.

Talking to his brother had taken his mind off the woman for a short time. But now with his brother gone, she was back full force.

"Kellie, I've got things to do. I'll talk to you tomorrow," he said to the woman who came strolling through the room, a rabbit in hand. He nodded to Angela, who was with her. Zach's daughter certainly had grown up into a pretty young lady. What had Tessa said? She was eighteen now? Nineteen? Unbelievable. He remembered her as a child.

"I'll see you in the morning, señor."

Going into his room where they had set up

a weight set, he carefully lowered himself to the bench.

Tessa.

A woman full of life, laughter and joy.

Tessa.

A woman full of secrets and surprises and new experiences.

Tessa.

The woman who could twist up his gut by simply taking his advice and going out on a date.

What was he? A fool? Suggesting she go out on a date?

The question wasn't what was he but why was this bothering him so much to see her going out with that other guy.

And knowing that was the one question he didn't want to answer, he turned to his weight set for comfort.

Chapter Twelve

"So, Tessa, now that dinner's over how about we go to a movie?"

Stan sounded so eager.

She hated to disappoint him. But Tessa had realized almost immediately that this was a mistake. She had never really wanted to go out on a date with this man. She'd simply done it in a fit of frustration at Drake.

"They have several new ones showing in the next county—"

"I really should go home." She smiled to soften the blow.

"Oh."

"I have guests. Both Kellie and Drake…" She trailed off.

Stan nodded. "Maybe this Friday then?"

"We'll have to see. I'm making such progress with Drake, I hate to leave him too much."

Stan's features darkened with his disappointment or, possibly, frustration. "Yeah," he muttered. "I'll take you home then."

"I'm sorry, Stan."

"Doesn't mean I'll stop trying," he said, and then standing, ushered her out of the small diner on Main Street and to his car. "Too bad you only live a few blocks away."

Strapping on her seat belt, she asked, "And why is that?"

"It'd give me more time to convince you to go to the movies if you lived out where those Slater brothers did."

"Liam and Drake," she corrected softly.

"Liam's a pretty funny guy. Drake's a lot more sober than I'd heard," Stan mused. He revved the engine and turned the car toward Tessa's home.

"I suppose he has reason to be," was all

Tessa said. Personally she thought Stan's comment a bit rude considering what Drake had been through. That comment had actually soured her evening and probably any other chances they'd had at going out together.

"Here we are."

Not waiting for him to get out and open her door, she slid out. Leaning down she said, "Thanks again. I'll see you tomorrow."

She closed the door before he could comment. Waving over her shoulder she headed for the house. Who was she kidding? His comment may have been a little crass, but her mind had been on Drake all night.

It was her guilt at leaving Drake as well as silently dwelling on him all night that assured her that fate had sealed her destiny as far as Stan was concerned.

He could have been a perfect gentleman, and she would not have gone back out with him.

She felt bad for agreeing to dinner with the man but tried to reassure herself he'd been so persistent and it hadn't hurt anything.

She couldn't believe she'd actually gone

out on a date. It had been too many years. It would have been much harder had Freckles not been there goading her. With her mind so preoccupied over the things Freckles had said, it'd taken nearly a half hour for her to remember how worried she was about dating.

When she'd remembered it was supposed to concern her, to her disbelief she found she wasn't the least bit anxious after all.

Probably because deep down she knew that this had been the one and only date she and Stan would have. It wouldn't be a repeat of Brea, California.

Quietly slipping the key into the lock she turned and pushed open the door. All was peaceful. Hubert didn't come to greet her, though Missy did.

Most of the lights in the house were out. It was barely nine in the evening but it looked as if everyone was already in bed.

As quietly as possible she shut the door behind her. Besides the ticking of the clock, the only other sound was Sam's nails and his wings as he tried to fly—then hit the floor with a thud. He tap-tap-tapped his way over toward her while she slipped off her jacket and hung up her purse. She grabbed the bird and slipped him onto her shoulder and then picked up Missy. Going into the kitchen she made sure Sam had his nighttime snacks and then put him in his cage and covered it.

She sat Missy down by her bowl and fed her before making sure the rabbits still had water.

After she slipped off her shoes, she left them near the entrance to the kitchen.

Her first indication that everyone was not asleep was when she got to the base of the stairs.

Thunk.

Listening carefully she tried to identify which way the sound came from. The hall or the room where Drake was now ensconced.

Thunk.

Again the noise. A metallic sound and definitely coming from the room off the kitchen, where Drake was. She headed back that way.

It sounded like weights, but the bigger weights were off-limits unless Stan was there assisting Drake so it couldn't be...

Ka-thunk-thunk.

It was!

She stopped in stunned disbelief, staring at the door. Her impulsive actions took over as she stormed right through the entrance.

The door banged with a thud from where she'd pushed it.

Drake's head turned from where he stood, the large barbells in his hands.

"What do you think you are doing?" she asked, shocked.

Drake glared. "Working out."

Taking a deep breath he concentrated. Then he lifted, doing the ritual breathing motions as he did. Tessa saw the sweat on his upper lip and biceps. His white T-shirt even looked damp against him, the tiny hairs around his ears curling.

Suddenly she realized she no longer saw the scar on his head. With the way he was standing—his side to her—she couldn't see the barbed wire marks. Being out in the sun every day, Drake wasn't even as pale as when he had first come.

This was definitely a full grown man standing there pumping iron. A very...fascinating man, she thought, then pushed those thoughts aside with disgust.

"You know better. You aren't supposed to do that unless Stan is here."

"Stan," Drake muttered low and lowered the bar back down to his thighs. "I don't need his help."

Breathing, he concentrated and hoisted the bar back up to his chest.

Tessa noted the lines of strain in his cheek. "You're pushing too hard. How long have you been at this?"

"Not long enough to forget," he said and lowered the bar again, a bit clumsily.

"What?" Confused, Tessa moved forward. "Forget what? Has something happened?"

Still not looking at her, he started back up with the bar.

Tessa realized immediately she'd gotten too close. Throwing up her arm, she tried to block the weights that were coming right at her.

She did, knocking them off balance.

Drake gasped as he lost his grip.

Tessa squeaked in dismay trying to catch her balance, but it was no good. She was going down.

Hard arms grabbed her.

Every bone in her body jarred forward into a solid body. Blindly reaching out, she grabbed at her rescuer.

With a thud and a very painful impact, she and Drake hit the floor.

Her only consolation was that her head was cradled against his chest.

"O-oh-oh," she moaned softly, her leg letting her know it didn't appreciate the weight. Cracking open an eye, she glanced around. "What happened to the weights? Are you okay?"

She rolled to her back, easing up on her elbows to look askance at him by her side…only to find him glaring at her.

"I'm fine. Perfectly fine. I would have been better had you not knocked those weights out of my hands."

She gasped. "*I* knocked them out? You weren't watching, either." She rolled back to her side and winced.

Drake pushed himself up to a sitting position, wincing as he did. Tessa didn't miss that. "You're hurt!" she exclaimed.

Reaching out she touched his shoulder, stopping him from standing.

That was her first mistake.

Tension charged the air.

His gaze snapped to hers.

His dark eyes filled with longing and interest. Tessa's couldn't help but respond.

Before she could think better, she made her second mistake. She leaned forward. That was all the invitation Drake needed. Turning, he slipped an arm around her and hauled her up against him. His lips came down on hers, fast and hard but then gentling as they touched.

Tessa's own arms went around him and she drowned in the all-consuming kiss they shared. How long had it been since she'd kissed anyone? Had anyone evoked the emotions this man was evoking right now? The tenderness, achy neediness, desire to share more...?

Just as fast as it had started, it ended. Suddenly she was sitting there, a good three feet between them, Drake breathing hard and looking at her as if she'd suddenly turned green on him.

"What?" she asked, still a bit dazed from the kiss.

"I apologize," he said shortly.

Tessa blinked. As she stared at him, his words finally registered. Finally she glared at him. "Well, I don't!"

Shoving painfully to her feet, she said, "Since you seem to feel so fine, I'll leave you to your self-torture."

Turning, she found almost immediately that she was in a lot worse pain than she'd realized.

"Tessa...wait!" Drake called out.

She had no choice. Gripping the door to keep upright, she used the excuse to turn and stare at him. She only hoped the vulnerability of what had just happened didn't show in her eyes. "What?" she asked, only her voice didn't come out venomous or angry as she'd wanted, but laced with tenderness. Swallowing, she forced herself not to show the roiling emotions inside her.

"I didn't mean it that way."

Tessa allowed her gaze to slide away from the man still sitting on the bedroom floor. "I didn't, either," she admitted.

A deep sigh escaped his lips. "It looks like we ought to do some talking, but not right now. Tomorrow, when our emotions are a bit more under control."

Tessa nodded. "I think tomorrow would be best."

"I'm glad you agree," he murmured.

She turned again to leave and he stopped her once more. "And Tessa?"

She didn't turn back to face him this time. "Yes?" she asked.

"I'm glad you're home early."

She nodded and slipped out the door, pulling it closed behind her.

Leaning against the wall, she rubbed her sore leg. And couldn't help the smile that curved her lips. Her entire being felt alive, vibrating with an excitement that she hadn't felt in years. All because of that man in there.

Quietly, she asked God, "What am I going to do?"

Chapter Thirteen

Drake sat in his wheelchair in the backyard, the soft rays of dawn lighting up the morning sky.

He hurt from head to toe. The pain was so bad, he'd had to call Stan last night to come help him. That fall had jarred bones in his body that didn't think they should be jarred. He was stiff. Stan assured him by tomorrow he'd be up and around again.

It had galled him to call Stan. All he could think about the entire time Stan had worked on him was that hours before Stan had been out with Tessa—on a date. And that was all Stan could talk about. How great it had gone.

The more Drake thought about it, the more he had second thoughts about talking with Tessa today. Last night with her in his arms, touching her lips, feeling her response, it had been easy to imagine a future with her.

Today in the early morning light all he could feel was that he was reaching for something that was impossible. Stan had insisted he use the wheelchair at least until this evening to make sure nothing was seriously wrong.

Being back in it, in some way, made his feelings of last night feel way too far-fetched. After all, what was he going to say to her? *I'm attracted to you, Tessa, and would like to explore our friendship and see if there's more. Maybe you'd even think about marrying an imperfect man such as me instead of the very healthy, handsome Stan who is very obviously interested in you....*

How long last night had he prayed and asked God why he was in this position? An hour, two? Three? He was too new to so many things.

He definitely wasn't new to some of those

feelings he'd had last night. He knew attraction when he felt it. But with Tessa it hadn't been lust. It had been…something much more he didn't even want to begin to think about.

That had terrified him. He'd known all of his old emotions but as Tessa had read to him from the Bible…he was a new man, a new creation. Evidently that meant all kinds of new feelings—including guilt for wanting Tessa as he did.

"Is it me, God? Or does she really return my feelings? Are they even right feelings for a woman?" He knew he'd never felt the way he did about Tessa. He was embarrassed to admit he was jealous of her date last night.

Jealousy!

How utterly ridiculous, he thought, exasperation filling him. Which brought him full circle. What had caused those feelings last night and why was he feeling them? Did he even have a right to act on what he was feeling?

"Good morning."

Drake heard the soft voice approaching

from behind. Grabbing the wheels, he turned the chair.

Tessa stood, wearing a pair of gray baggy pants and an equally baggy peach top, hands clasped in front of her. "How are you this morning? Kellie tells me after I went to bed you had to call Stan."

He nodded. "Because I'm so sore he insists that I stay in this wheelchair today—at least the first half of the day."

"And you don't mind?" she asked.

"Actually, with the way I feel, I don't mind." He motioned to the small table where Kellie was setting up breakfast.

Tessa hesitated and then turned.

Drake knew why she'd hesitated as he watched her. "You were hurt last night!"

Limping to the table, she brushed away his concern with a wave of her hand. "It's not anything new. Occasionally the hip injury where I was crushed from the earthquake..."

Drake moved his chair forward positioning it at a right angle to Tessa. "Why didn't you say something last night?"

She smiled, not meeting his eyes. "Just like you said something to me?"

"Touché," he admitted. Bowing his head he offered a prayer for the food put before them. Then they began to eat.

"Your flexibility and movements have gotten much better," Tessa commented quietly before taking a bite of her eggs.

"And your pets are learning to steer clear of me," he said before picking up his juice and sipping it.

Watching Tessa purposely avoid looking him in the eye bothered him. "Tessa," he said softly, determined to draw her eyes to him. "Look at me."

Setting her fork down, she finally, hesitantly—though she tried to look casual about it—lifted her eyes to meet his.

That zing of attraction and understanding shot right through him at the touch of her gaze. He swallowed. This was going to be a lot tougher than he'd thought. "Do I need to apologize again for last night?" he asked carefully.

Her cheeks bloomed with color. "No. Of course not. I—well..." she sighed.

"Don't want to be involved with someone in a wheelchair?"

"No!" Shocked, her gaze shot back to his. "That's not it at all! It's just that after Brea..."

"Good morning, children."

The sound of Julian "Hawk" McCade's voice made Drake and Tessa turn their heads. Drake thought Julian and Freckles couldn't have had worse timing. He wanted to tell them to leave and wait five more minutes until he found out *what* about Brea had to do with what happened last night.

"Children?" he asked instead.

"Hawk is trying to make a joke," Freckles said, smiling. Both were dressed with lab coats, obviously on their way to work.

"Please. Have a seat. We have plenty," Tessa offered.

Freckles took a seat though she waved her hand at the food. "Couldn't handle it this early," she said to Tessa and then turned to Drake. "We heard you had a fall last night."

Drake sighed. "Stan?"

Julian nodded. "Dr. Coleson asked us to stop by and have a look on our way in. So what happened?"

He cleared his throat.

Tessa glanced down at her plate, chewing on a piece of toast, her cheeks shading darker red at his question. Julian didn't miss the action. Turning a curious eye to Freckles, he grinned. "An accident?" he asked of Drake, his gaze finally turning to him.

Drake said coolly, "I was working out with the weights. I lost my balance and fell."

"I tripped him," Tessa added.

Julian nodded. "Stan said he worked on you half the night. He wanted to make sure you weren't too stiff and sore. How are you feeling today?"

Drake shrugged. "As would be expected— stiff and sore."

Julian crossed his legs. "I'd like to have you come into the clinic or the hospital to Dr. Coleson if you prefer later today. Can that be arranged?"

"I can see he gets there," Tessa said.

Drake, who had opened his mouth to say he could call his brother and see, promptly closed it. Though he was surprised Tessa had offered he certainly wasn't going to argue about taking a ride with her. "I'd prefer the clinic," Drake said, finding he liked the two younger doctors and their easygoing attitude better than the older man.

"Hawk will be in during the afternoon. I'm working this morning. He has some classes he has to teach at the hospital—outpatient classes. So make it around two if you can."

"That sounds good." Casting a look at Tessa, Drake added, "She's in pain as well. Seems an old injury flared up. Think you could take a look at her while we're there?"

Tessa glared at him.

"What happened?" Julian asked, concerned.

"Your accident," Freckles murmured. "You reinjured yourself?"

She cast an exasperated glance at Drake then nodded to her friend. "I'm afraid so. I probably just need anti-inflammatories again."

"We'll see about that," Freckles murmured. "I'll make sure you have an appointment as well. You don't want to end up back in therapy again."

"No. No, I don't."

Finishing up his eggs and toast, Drake pushed his plate away.

"Let me push you in while we talk," Julian said standing to his feet and moving behind the wheelchair.

Tessa saw his long-suffering look at her, almost a warning that their conversation wasn't over.

"What was that all about?" Freckles asked as soon as Drake was out of earshot.

Tessa shrugged a delicate shrug. "Nothing, really. It was just an accident."

"That's not what I was talking about. I saw the looks that passed between you two. Something more than a simple accident happened between you two last night." Eagerly Freckles leaned forward. "So, spill it, Tessa."

Tessa rolled her eyes and sighed. "You leave me no secrets, you know that, don't you?"

Freckles chuckled. "I enjoy a good story. I'm a romantic at heart."

Tessa couldn't help but laugh at Freckles's enthusiasm. "I wish I could be as positive as you are that something good happened. I...he...well—" she picked up her cup and sipped her drink "—I...he...we sorta kissed last night."

Freckles chuckled. "Before or after Stan left?"

"Freckles!" Tessa tried to sound shocked, but couldn't help the nervous laughter that escaped. "It didn't work out between Stan and me. It did show me that going out was certainly something interesting rather than terrifying, but there just wasn't anything there."

Freckles patted her hand. "Don't worry. Go on. How did you end up in a situation with Drake to kiss him?"

Tessa dropped her gaze. "He was working out with the weights. I went in to chastise him because I knew he wasn't supposed to use those without supervision. We ended up tripping and falling. I'm not sure what happened after that except..."

She trailed off, not sure how to put it. Freckles filled in for her, ''Except you just got one of the most shocking kisses that you never expected, right?''

Tessa wrinkled her nose. ''Shocking…?''

''Totally surprising, out of this world—''

''I know what you meant,'' Tessa interrupted. ''I just don't think I've ever heard that word in that context before.''

''Stop avoiding the answer.''

''I think it shocked both of us,'' Tessa muttered.

''You weren't ready for it, were you?'' Freckles asked sympathetically.

''I'm not ready for any of this. I haven't dated in over five years. I've had a hysterectomy, I'm a danger. Why would any man risk himself to date me?''

Realizing what she had said, Tessa groaned. She knew Freckles wouldn't let that pass by. And she didn't.

''Maybe because he's only had eyes for you since the day he met you. And you haven't been able to look anywhere else either? And maybe because, honey, this isn't the past. You deserve a fresh start.''

''I...I don't know. I don't want anything to happen...''

''What?'' Freckles asked when Tessa didn't finish the sentence.

''Nothing,'' Tessa whispered.

Squeezing her hand, Freckles said, ''You're going to have to be honest sooner or later. This man cares for you whether you've seen it or not. You don't want to lose him.''

Tessa agreed with Freckles. She didn't want to lose him. But then, did she even have a right to endanger the man either? She was simply being superstitious. *Forgive me, Father. You can handle that area. It's not my job to protect him,* she said silently, but then had to wonder if that was true.

''Well then, Tessa. Trust God. I'm going on out to the clinic. I'll see you at two. Please, though, if you care for Drake, trust him.''

Finally Tessa nodded. ''I'll see what I can do on that end.''

"That's all I can ask," Freckles said and rose to leave. "Be good."

As she watched Freckles go inside to collect her husband, she wondered just what she'd meant by that last statement.

Be good?

With that in mind, she headed in the opposite direction to take a stroll into town, thinking that this was the best way she could be good where Drake Slater was concerned.

Chapter Fourteen

"**Y**ou are sure you don't mind stopping by the line shack?"

Tessa smiled. "Of course I don't, Drake. I would love to see your ranch, and I understand your need to see where it all happened. And since your appointment went so well…"

"I still can't believe they said I could go home within the week."

"I'm happy for you."

Drake glanced over at Tessa, studying the way her brown hair had slipped from the clip and curled around her face. Her high cheekbones, curve of her jaw, pert nose stood out against that dark hair. He wanted to reach over and touch it, tell her all was okay. She'd seemed elated and saddened with the report Dr. McCade had given him.

"About this morning…"

The smile slipped.

"I find you attractive." Drake had decided when Tessa had disappeared for so long today he might as well tell her what he felt. Never before would he have been so obvious to someone about his feelings if he didn't think they returned them. Nor would he have cared particularly how the woman would react.

But being a Christian had opened up an entirely new way of thinking. He still didn't understand it completely but with the stories Tessa had presented him, stories from the Bible, written on a level he could read to reinforce what they read each day, he was learning and discovering new things. What he hadn't told her was that he had actually started reading a Bible and could make out ninety percent of it now.

She had worked hard with him. Maybe that was part of why he wanted to be so open.

That and the fact that he had this love just pouring out of him. He wanted to be just plain honest with her, like he'd never been with a woman before.

"I was afraid you did…. Oh, Drake," she whispered.

Anguish laced her voice.

"If you don't return those feelings, Tessa, all you have to do is say so. I would understand—"

"But I do," she said softly, low.

Drake stared.

"Why such torment then? I don't think you're shallow enough to worry about my scars or my limp. And I certainly hope you don't think I'm shallow enough to worry about the fact you can't have children."

A near sob escaped her lips.

"Tessa, I'm sorry. I didn't mean that to sound so crass."

"No." She shook her head. "It's not that. I just…well after Michael made his feelings clear about my loss I wasn't sure I'd find a man that would ever be able to accept me as I am. But…I just…"

Gripping the wheel, she glanced off across the desert-like, rocky area of land. What did she see in the cacti and scrub brush, the hills and the mesquite? He doubted she even noted any of it; rather, she most likely still dwelt on whatever had driven her away this morning.

"Yes?" he asked. "Tell me, Tessa."

"I just don't think…"

As she glanced back at him he saw the worry and strain in her features. "I couldn't stand it if you were hurt."

Well now, he thought. That wasn't exactly what he'd been expecting. "Care to explain that?"

Releasing the wheel she rubbed a hand over her eyes. "There's something I haven't told you."

He had gathered that much, he thought, waiting for her to continue. "What?" he goaded teasingly. "You sunbathed nude and got caught on one of those beaches?" He thought he sounded outrageous but she didn't respond.

Tessa turned as pale as the white sands of New Mexico. So pale, that Drake was certain she was going to pass out. "No. But I'll never have children."

He stared, unable to think of what to say. Finally, he reached out to touch her arm. He felt a real fool for goading her as he had. It might have made her confess something she hadn't really wanted to confess.

She covered her mouth in dismay.

"Shush. It's okay." He tried to reassure her, the pain in her eyes eating at his gut.

"No! It's not. I've never...I can't..."

Tessa's voice sounded wild, frantic as she gripped the wheel. She swerved to avoid a turtle on the rarely used road.

Alarmed, Drake grabbed the dashboard. "Tessa. Honey, you have to talk about this. You obviously hadn't planned to tell me, but this..."

"I can't Drake! I just can't."

"Why not?"

Frantically she shook her head. Drake wondered if she realized the car weaved with the movement of her head. The way she gripped the wheel...she was going to get them both killed.

Boy, had he triggered something within her. "Why not, Tessa?"

"Because…"

He glanced out the window to make sure they were still on the road. Tessa seemed to gain some control as she took a deep breath. "I shouldn't have brought it up. Really."

Tessa's face had paled even more. "Why are you telling me now?" he asked gently.

"I won't let you think I'm…that I…" Shuddering, she took a deep breath. "I'm not whole. So you might as well forget any thoughts of me being the perfect one for you. I can't have children."

The bitterness in her voice filled Drake with compassion. "Oh, baby," he whispered low. "Pull over now."

She didn't argue, turning toward the small shack that sat just ahead off the road. She then killed the engine. Breathing a quick sigh of relief, Drake reached across the small compact car and hooked an arm around her. "You haven't talked about this much with anyone, have you?"

The woman in his arms was trembling as

if she'd been struck with sudden palsy. Her entire body quivered as she worked to keep control.

"I don't want to remember it," she whispered.

"That's why you haven't dated anyone...."

"Oh, but you're wrong!" she said, and he could hear the tears coming. "I tried but, you see, I felt honesty should come first. And as soon as the men found out that there was no future, they either propositioned me or left me. I don't plan to go through that again."

She burst into tears just before shoving away and bolting out of the car.

Stunned, Drake quickly shoved his own door open and, as quickly as possible and ignoring the pain, hauled himself out and strode toward the line shack where she'd disappeared. "Tessa, honey?" he called pushing the door open.

She stood, her head down, near the small window, a tissue in her hand. "I'm so embarrassed for you to see me like this," she whispered. "This is so utterly stupid! I just…it's hard to warn you, you understand, because I do have feelings for you.''

Drake crossed the room in two strides. Turning her, he pulled her into his arms and simply held her. He had never been through a horror of the type Tessa had just said. How did one survive an earthquake to find out she would never have kids? He was pretty sure that's what she was getting at. It all made sense now, including why that jerk had deserted her and married someone else. He wasn't sure how he would handle it, or how he would have coped back then, but now… "It wasn't your fault, baby," he whispered, holding her close. "You can't carry that burden."

"But it was my fault. If I hadn't thought about getting involved with him maybe it wouldn't have happened. Maybe God was punishing me for rebelling against Him or maybe it was because…"

"Enough," he whispered low. Drake rubbed his hands up and down her back, working to calm the tender young woman in his arms. Not having any idea what to do he

began to sing a song he often heard her sing
that he'd picked up in church over the past
few weeks. It was a simple song about God
being there through the storms, providing for
and lifting up His children, but it did the job.
The tender spirit of God filled the shack and
a gentle peace floated upon the wings of love,
surrounding them, easing the pain, giving
peace to Tessa.

When she turned around and leaned into
his chest, he said low, "If I remember what
was written in the Bible I read the other day,
you can't be God, Tessa. You don't know the
mind of God and can't guess why those
things happened. You just have to accept and
grow…"

Tessa blinked away the tears, reaching for
a tissue in her pocket. "I know. The Word
says that but sometimes it's so hard."

Glancing back out the window, she asked,
quietly, "This is where the accident happened?"

He wrapped his arms from behind her and
rested his chin on her head. "About a quarter
of a mile away. We keep our bull in this pas-

ture. We'll have to get a new one now since Liam said he'd planned to either sell or put this one down. But yeah, I was out riding the fence, checking out things. We're both injured in some ways, Tessa. You were hurt emotionally and went through things I can't even imagine. But I can have the faith here, in my heart, and be there for you until you can stand on your own, if you let me. Just like you've stood for me over the past weeks when I was worried about things my brother had done or said. And we both just have to trust God like the Bible reads." Drake squeezed her gently. "Isn't that where faith comes in, Tessa? You just have to believe God is in control?"

She wiped her eyes and shook her head.

She turned and glanced up. The last traces of tears gone, the only evidence left being her red nose and the shocked gaze in her red-rimmed eyes, she asked, "You quoting the sermon to me and scripture you read in the Bible?"

He grinned. "I was saving it for a special

time. But Tessa, I have read nearly an entire book of the Bible.''

''Oh, Drake!'' She leaned forward and hugged him, squeezing him tightly and allowing her pleasure and excitement to manifest itself in her actions. ''Why hadn't you told me?''

''As I said, I wanted to wait until just the right time. I guess now was the best time possible.'' He shook his head. ''Now, however, back to you,'' he said, sternly. ''You think I can't take care of myself or that God can't take care of me?''

''Of course you can,'' Tessa muttered.

''Then it's me? You just don't care for me?''

''Yes, I do,'' she argued, then promptly blushed.

Allowing a self-satisfied smile to curve his lips, he said, ''I've been waiting for weeks now to hear you say that.''

She groaned. ''You still have a ladies' man in you, Drake Slater.''

He sobered. ''Only for you, Tessa Stanridge. Only for you.'' And only her. How could he tell her just what she meant to him? She was his life. He felt for her things he couldn't even put into words. He wanted to weep each time he touched her, weep with the simple joy of touching someone who felt so right. It didn't make sense, but he was certain this woman was put in his path by God. She was exactly what he needed and could have hoped for and, as far as he was concerned, he was the right man for her.

"You haven't asked me if having children is that important, Tessa," he said softly.

A glimmer of surprise touched her gaze just before her features softened. "You're the oldest, though. I would think you'd want…"

When she trailed off, he shook his head. "A child is a child. If we want children, we can adopt. There're plenty of kids out there who need parents."

Fresh tears spilled over. "You don't mean that. He wouldn't be of your flesh…"

Drake grinned roguishly. "*She* wouldn't have to be of my flesh, baby."

He smiled at her, then slowly he sobered. Now came the most important part. He wasn't sure how to ask it except to just say it and see what she replied. "So since that doesn't matter, just like my own scars don't matter, tell me why you won't consider dating me?"

Playing with the tissue in her hand, she stared at it. He had learned her nervous actions well over the last few weeks. This one, as well as nibbling her lip, tilting her head, crossing her legs back and forth...

"Maybe because you haven't asked me."

Hope soared in his chest. "Then if I asked you?" he queried.

"I would want to Drake but I'm just..."

He didn't like that pause. His heart doubled its beat with that tiny pause. "Yes?" he asked warily.

"I guess I'm just scared. I—you're different from Stan. The only reason I went out with him is because you made me mad," she confessed, her lower lip pouting out in consternation.

Drake burst into deep, rich chuckles, relief spreading through every part of his body. "And to think I was jealous of your date."

"You told me to go!" she argued, her

voice rising with shock and outrage at his re-action.

"But I didn't think you would!" he retorted, grinning from ear to ear. "So what about a date, Tessa?" he asked, grinning.

His heart expanded with love. Yes, love. Not friendship or a desire to simply date this woman, but full-blown love. "Trust me, Tessa. Nothing is going to happen."

She twisted the tissue. "I want to believe, Drake. I mean until the date with Stan all I could see in Stan was the possessive attitude of Michael. I realize now I was wrong but…"

"But what?" he asked patiently. He had all the time in the world now that he had defined just what it was in his heart that kept him awake thinking about this woman day and night.

"But when I look at you," she whispered. "I don't see Michael at all. I see someone growing older and wishing they'd had their own kids. It's bad enough, the injuries that may make it impossible for you to be totally mobile again, but then to have this heaped upon you…"

Stunned once again, he stared at her. How did he fight a ghost like that? "I don't care if we have children, honey," he reiterated. "And I promise you, I won't ever get tired of being with you and I will be mobile again." *Heavenly Father, she's still worried about me turning bitter.* Shaking his head, he silently continued, *Any ideas how to convince her I am going to be normal and not end up old and bitter?* He prayed but then decided, when in doubt of what to do, turn on his Slater charm. Surely she would see the truth in his eyes, feel the truth when he held her. It was the only way *he* could think to convince her. Honesty. He'd told her the first day they should be up-front and honest with each other.

He wondered what any of his old friends would think of that. Him being honest with a woman. Actually, he knew what they would think—that he'd lost his mind and was crazy. But at the moment it didn't matter. He was a new creature in God and he was in love with Tessa Stanridge.

Shifting, he slipped his arms around her.

Allowing his defenses to fall, he let her see what shone in his eyes, let her see the honesty as he said, "Tessa, I'm going to confess something to you right now."

Her eyes widened in surprise, warming him. He saw that she wasn't used to others being so honest and it thrilled him he could be. He also liked the way her mind obviously drifted from her fears to the fact that he held her now.

"I, um…" she mumbled, but trailed off, her gaze touching his cheeks, his nose, his eyes, his lips.

"I've fallen in love with you," he whispered, the ache within him swelling with his need to tell her all. "Baby, I don't know when it happened. I just know, watching you today, it suddenly dawned on me that I love you."

"Oh, Drake," she said softly, nibbling her lip in sudden worry. Her gaze touched his features again before sliding away.

He wouldn't let her get away with that. She needed loving. She needed to know she wasn't alone, that he loved her as she was, that God loved her as she was and that he could easily take care of himself—the last he was leaving to God. Pulling her into his embrace, he held her close. "I don't know how you feel about me, Tess. That scares me. This is a first for me, honey."

Her tiny body trembled in his arms. He felt the warmth of her tears as they wet the front of his shirt. He had to say Tessa was certainly one to show her emotions—another thing he loved about her. He simply held her, not sure what else to say when, quietly, her alto voice broke the silence of the shack. "I—I—love you," she whispered low into his shoulder.

Joy burgeoned anew within him. She loved him. He was certain his heart was going to explode. Had it only been less than a year ago he had been drinking and carousing and dying of loneliness inside? Had it only been less than six months ago that not half a mile from here on his back he had gone as far down as he could and discovered his Savior? And now, less than three months out of the hospital, and he was hearing the words he so wanted to hear from the woman he loved—a woman he hadn't even known existed until a short time before. God certainly did work miracles, he thought, peacefully. "Do you?" he asked, easing back to meet her eyes, needing to help her reaffirm what was going on within her own battleground.

"But I can't," she whispered and he heard the torment in her voice. "What if—?"

"Shush," he said, placing a finger over her lips. "You can't predict the future. Just as I can't promise that *you* won't end up upset that you can't have kids and leave me. Think of the song we sang the other day about how sweet to hold that newborn baby and know he'll face uncertain days? That's us, Tessa. God doesn't guarantee we won't go through things, but He does guarantee we won't go through them alone. I want you to go through my trials and I want to go through your trials and I want us both to go through our joys together for the rest of our lives." Not giving her a chance to respond, he leaned down and kissed her, putting all of the love he had in his heart into the kiss.

She hesitated and then melted into his

sweet embrace, returning the gentle, touching and attracting embodiment of his love.

Realizing he was starting to feel more than just his overwhelming love for her and the fact that something, some noise, was niggling at the back of his mind that there was something else going on within the radius of their private area, he stepped back.

Just in time, too. The echoing sound of a car engine shutting down caught his attention just as the door to the tiny shack they currently occupied burst open. Dark roiling sky painted the background along with a second vehicle just beyond the metal cattle guard and fence. The vehicle belonged to the man who stood in the doorway—a man that Drake didn't expect to see. "Stan?" he asked, surprised to see the man standing there.

Chapter Fifteen

Dazed, Tessa turned her gaze to the door. She smelled the crisp rain, felt the humid, cool breeze that sent a mild chill down her spine and finally focused on the person standing in front of her. "Stan?" she asked, confused. "What are you doing here?"

Tessa was still trying to separate the feelings she'd just been experiencing with the reality before her. Dusty remains from where Stan had obviously driven up drifted in, tickling her nose.

Turning, she sneezed.

"I was on my way out to the ranch, where

you two were supposedly headed. I had come out to the clinic to check on your appointment and how my patient was doing.''

He cast a dark look at Drake. ''Instead, I noticed a dust trail turning onto this road so I followed it.''

Tessa accepted Drake's hankie and dotted at her eyes. ''I don't understand—''

''This is the southwest corner of Slater property,'' Drake interrupted coolly.

Glancing from one to the other a sinking feeling filled Tessa. It was happening again, just like last time. Feelings of déjà vu filled her, engulfing her, chilling her to the bone.

''Why are you hanging out with this loser?'' Stan demanded. ''I thought you wanted better—''

''That's enough, Stan,'' Drake growled low. ''As I said, this is Slater property.''

A wave of dizziness assailed Tessa as her past and present collided. Michael had confronted her just like this and told her he was marrying someone else. What was it with men and her?

Stan snorted, interrupting those awful

memories that she suddenly realized weren't so awful anymore. She was back to the moment. "Yeah, sure it's enough. Because you have her where you want her. We've been friends longer than you have any right to know. She went out on a date with me and intimated we'd be going out again...."

Drake's hands fisted.

"Stop it!" Tessa demanded, trembling. She wouldn't stand by and say nothing again. Before she might have been too stunned as her former fiancé had hurled insults, accusations and finally turned violent, but she couldn't stand still this time. Not now, not when she realized she truly did love Drake. This wasn't the rebellious lust like she'd felt for Michael, but a true, deep, abiding love that had touched her heart and had integrated itself into her inner-most being. This man was the man God had called for her just as sure as she believed Michael was the one put in her path to trip her up and play on her other desires, just as much as she was put in his path as well. "I'm not interested in dating you, Stan. I don't know where you got the idea that I was exclusively yours—"

"But you said more than once we'd go out. I've been waiting, Tessa—" He started forward.

Shaking her head, she thrust out her hand stopping him in his tracks. "No, Stan. I know you have been interested for a long time. I wasn't ready before. I didn't realize that it was Drake who had actually made me ready. But he did. Through him I've learned to trust again. I didn't know how to tell you that the other night." She dabbed at her watering eyes again.

"I don't believe you, Tessa." Stan's voice took on a whining quality. "You and I have shared friendship, cards, you've accepted it when I brought flowers... It's only been since *he* arrived that you've changed."

Drake stepped forward. "You heard her, Stan. Be a gentleman and bow out politely."

Drake's hand, drifting to and touching her back, gave Tessa the added strength to say, "I'm sorry, Stan. I should have said something earlier but I just didn't know you were this serious.''

"You'd rather go around with someone that has a reputation like he does, Tessa, instead of someone like me? Why didn't you tell me? I could have played the ladies' man, whatever you wanted. But you didn't want that. Going to church and acting so upright..."

Tessa gasped at his indications.

"I think you'd better go." Drake's voice had taken on a coldly flat tone that caused a shiver to run through Tessa. Lifting the hankie she started to dab at her eyes again.

Stan's gaze darted from one to the other, then he lunged forward. Gripping Tessa's arm he jerked her forward. "Not until I convince Tessa she's being ridiculous."

"Stan!" She could only gasp out in her shock. She dropped the hankie and worked to stay on her feet.

Drake shouted and rushed forward but Stan was faster, hauling her out the front door.

Stumbling, she grabbed at Stan to keep her balance.

"You have to listen to me," Stan began. "You don't understand. The feelings you have for this guy are simply because you're caring for him—"

Tessa wrenched, working to free herself from his surprisingly strong grip. "That's not true. Stan, are you crazy? Let me go!"

"Let her go!" Drake echoed, limping forward amazingly fast, considering he was in pain. He lunged himself and snagged Stan, gripping him by the other arm.

What she lacked in strength, Drake had evidently developed as he shoved Stan away, looping an arm around Tessa as he did.

Tessa sucked in a sharp breath of pain.

"Watch out!" Stan yelled, turning pale and then scrambling to his feet. Before they could adjust to the change from his hostile to fearful attitude, he was crossing the cattle guard toward his car.

Tessa stared confused. "What in the...?"

Drake stiffened. "He was suppose to be put down or sold," Drake muttered under his voice.

"What?" Tessa started to turn but Drake held her firm.

"Don't move, Tessa, honey. You know the bull that put me in the hospital?"

"Yeah. You said he was…put down or…" She trailed off, just knowing what was coming. Oh, how she knew. Yes, she knew all right. Out of all the possibilities in the world, there was one that just couldn't happen—which meant it would. "It's not dead?"

"Bingo. The animal wasn't…" he started grimly.

"Oh no," she whispered, low.

"…exactly," he finished.

"Will he let us just walk out?" Very, very slowly she turned her head until she could catch a glimpse of what awaited them.

She wished she hadn't when she saw the huge animal. "He's the biggest cow I've ever seen," she said, the hair on the back of her neck coming to attention.

"He's not a cow, honey. He's a bull."

"He's one of the ugliest bulls I've ever seen," she whispered. "Even if he is the first one."

Tessa shivered, staring at the bull. He easily weighed more than both of them put together. What had she read once? That these things could weigh over twelve hundred pounds? This ugly black animal with the long white horns looked at least that heavy.

She would bet if the bull and a truck got in a contest as to which one could stand up the longest, this animal would win over the tons of steel.

"Hurry! Get out of there!" Stan called out from the other side of the fence, waving frantically.

"He didn't leave?" Tessa asked, surprised.

"We'll discuss that later, honey. We just need to get out of here now."

"How?"

The bull, which had been staring at them, snorted, the sound causing goose bumps to rise on Tessa's arms. He pawed the ground once, his beady eyes boring into them with challenge.

"On three, Tessa. I am going to push you toward the fence one way and rush the other way, drawing its attention."

Tessa gasped, her hand tightening on Drake's arm. "You can't do that!" she whispered low and furious.

The bull stiffened, lifting its head.

"Tessa!" he warned low. "I love you. I am not going to let happen to you what happened to me. Trust me."

"I—I—can't. I just can't. Oh, Drake. I love you. I can't let you do this!" Thunder sounded.

"Trust God," he whispered. "He saved me once with an angel of the Lord and He can do it again."

She hesitated, feeling as if the entire world had slowed in anticipation of what was about to happen. "I love you, Drake. I love you. I love you. Please, please, please get out of this alive," she chanted. A lightning bolt cut across the sky.

"One..."

"I'll even marry you to prove it," she added, her teeth chattering.

"Two..."

"And eat cow every night!" she said on a

near sob. Thunder resounded as the storm finally announced its presence.

"Three!" He shoved her. "Go! Go! Go! *Go!*"

She stumbled toward the fence one way. "Help him, help him, help him, God!" she cried out, running for all she was worth.

She heard Drake take off the other way, yelling and whistling. The wind picked up carrying the sounds off from her.

Sobbing, she raced toward the fence. "Help him!" she cried out toward the sky.

A loud boom echoed, nearly deafening her.

She gasped, her mind unable to register the sound. Again it sounded, and again.

She dove for the cattle guard, sailing over it toward safety, hitting the ground, rolling just as another report sounded.

Coming to rest on her back she realized she was lying right up against a pair of legs clad in white. Following them up she found Stan standing there, a rifle to his shoulder as he squeezed off one more round.

Gasping for breath, she rolled over and up on to her hands and knees looking, searching.

"There!" she pointed near the fence. "He's hurt!"

The bull was down in death throes but Drake lay motionless just outside the fence.

Sucking in a breath she scrambled up, just as the skies opened up and let loose with a crack of thunder that would have easily deafened her had the rifle not already taken care of the duty.

Ignoring the pain in her leg and her scraped up hands, she raced to Drake's side. The skies opened up and rain pelted them as she dropped down by him. "Drake! Oh, Drake!" she cried out, her hands hovering over him with fear that if she touched him and found him dead she would die herself.

"That bull certainly made his displeasure known."

The muttered words spoken into the grassy area where Drake's face was buried had never sounded sweeter in her life.

"What happened?" She couldn't help but sob and throw herself down on top of him.

He grunted. Managing to roll, he slipped his arms around her.

Tessa didn't mind the rain, didn't mind the thunder or lightning. She didn't care that they were getting soaked. She didn't care about anything but the man in her arms.

"He butted me in the, er, rear and I went sailing. I landed on the barbed wire again."

Gasping, she pushed back to find there was a definite line of injury across his abdomen. "It...I think it's superficial," she whispered, her fingers touching the blood before she started trembling all over again.

Drake pushed up and shifted back against a wooden beam, careful not to hit the wires of the fence. Hauling Tessa into his lap he hugged her close, which she didn't mind at all. "You're bleeding, Drake," she whispered, and then laughed before a sob escaped.

He stiffened.

She glanced up to see what was the matter and realized he glanced past her.

She turned her head to find Stan there, rifle in hand, staring at them.

Tessa felt every bit of color drain from her face.

Stan cocked his head oddly at her.

Drake's voice rumbled, "I have you to thank. If you hadn't had that rifle in the back of your car, that bull would have gotten me before I could push myself the rest of the way over the fence."

Tessa felt the vibration as Drake spoke, heard the words, but her mind was sluggish. Pushing the wet strands of hair from her face, she glanced up at Stan.

Again she noted he held the rifle. This time, however, she noted he didn't hold it threateningly. It was resting in his left hand at his side.

In his eyes was a look of anguish.

"You really do love him, Tessa."

In that moment it dawned on her that Stan truly did have feelings for her, feelings she had never realized. When he'd brought her flowers, stopping by to check on her she'd thought it was in friendship. He'd meant it as more. When he'd drop her a card in the mail, a silly little card about their friendship, he'd meant it as more.

Stan's pain touched her. "Yes, Stan, I do. I'm sorry."

He nodded. His gaze left her and turned to Drake. "Will you need help?"

Drake's hands rubbed her shoulders. "Could you go tell my brother what happened? We'll be along shortly."

With a curt nod Stan turned. He hesitated then glanced back. His gaze met Tessa's. "Goodbye, Tessa," he said and then strode off.

Tessa watched him get in his car. He revved the engine and then was heading down the road back toward the main ranch house.

"He really cared for you," Drake murmured.

"I didn't feel the same way," Tessa whispered.

His arms closed around her pulling her back against his chest. "I know, honey." Kissing her next to her ear, he whispered, "And I know God protected us today."

She nodded. "I do, too. Oh, Drake, I've been so selfish, only seeing my past and what had happened to me. In the scheme of things it's like we're these tiny birds trying to take on a cat while someone is standing about to pull the cat out of our way. We see the cat but not the one behind the cat who has it on the leash. Or in this case, we see the enemy but not the power of God who can keep that enemy in check.''

"I've been trying to tell you that, honey. Think about it. God did save us. He used Stan as His angel of mercy.''

"Oh! Yes!'' She turned and slipped her arms around him, holding him close. "I'm slow to learn,'' she whispered.

"But you do learn, in more areas than just this.''

Hearing the teasing in his voice, she smiled. "I meant what I said about loving you, you know.''

His big hand cupped the back of her head. Leaning down, he kissed her on the temple. "I know you did.''

Arrogance touched his voice. She would allow him that. "I guess it was when I said I loved you when you were counting, huh?''

"Nah,'' he murmured and moved his lips down to just below her ear.

"When I told you I'd marry you?'' Tessa

closed her eyes and turned her head so she could meet his lips in a gentle kiss of affirmation and love.

"No, not even then."

She opened her eyes, blinking the warm afternoon rain away. Studying the strange smile on his face, she finally asked, "Well when, then, did you decide I loved you?"

Drake reached out, touched her chin with his hand and rubbed a thumb over her lower lip. A Cheshire cat grin spread across his face and he murmured, "When you promised to eat meat every night for the rest of your life."

The sound of an echoing shout could be heard that day for miles around as Tessa Stanridge and Drake Slater discussed the future.

* * * * *

Dear Reader,

These past two years have flown as I've written for
Love Inspired, and I just want to thank you for the
hundreds of letters I've received. So many have blessed
and touched me and my family that I pray God's
blessings to you all.

I think that's probably what inspired this current story.
We, as humans, often look at the outside, what someone
does or does not do in the public eye, if they are good-
looking or bad-looking, if they say or act in the right
way. Each letter I got reminded me over and over how
we truly don't know each other and what is in someone
else's heart. We may never know. But God knows. He
sees in our hearts and knows us. The best part of all is
He forgives us. If we all could only see as God sees—
through eyes of love—think how much better our world
would be.

This story deals with Tessa Stanridge, who has gone
through medical problems as well as emotional hurts,
and Drake Slater, a brand-new Christian who was saved
at the instant he almost died. We see through his eyes
of love, the first love that God gives each of us as
Christians. We get to experience the world, not perfect,
certainly not the way most people would want, but still
with God's love helping us along.

I hope you enjoy the silly fun things Tessa and Drake go
through as together they discover healing for the souls
and bodies and love for their hearts. As always, you can
contact me at P.O. Box 207, Slaughter, LA 70777.

Until later: blessings,

Cheryl Wolverton

If you enjoyed reading
HEALING HEARTS,
you'll love
A HUSBAND TO HOLD,
the fifth book in Cheryl Wolverton's
HILL CREEK, TEXAS *series.*

For a sample of
A HUSBAND TO HOLD,
just turn the page....

Chapter One

September 1997

"Ashes to ashes. Dust to dust..."

Leah Hawkins heard the words as she stared at the casket before her. It was over, done with, finished.

She wanted to cry, but the tears would not come. She was still too much in shock over what she'd discovered only three days ago when the person had showed up at her door, just before she'd been told the horrible news about her husband.

"...an honorable man who served as one of our city's finest..."

Honorable? She stared at the casket as the preacher rambled on. She had thought her husband honorable. Everyone in church had thought him honorable. Otherwise he wouldn't have been a deacon. Even Zachary's finest had thought him honorable or he wouldn't have had his job.

"...commit him now to a heavenly father..."

Commit him to God? Leah could only hope God would have mercy on his soul. How she prayed God would have mercy. She hoped. She prayed, but she could not cry.

The horrible tales—backed up with evidence—the person had imparted to her that awful day still filled her mind.

"...and we finally ask, Almighty God, that You find the murderer of this fine respected citizen, this loving husband and father, this upright Christian..."

Leah's heart beat faster. Looking down into the casket at her husband's still, peaceful face she thought, *the pastor can pray for someone to find your murderer, Joseph, but I already know who murdered you.*

Glancing up, her gaze riveted to the man standing at the opposite end of the procession. He was a man in uniform, wearing gloves, teary-eyed and supposedly mourning with the others around him. A pallbearer, he was well known himself. The press had interviewed him about her husband and a drug dealer— the very dealer who had been at her door just before she'd heard of her husband's death— who had been found dead in a Scotlandville Alley. What would the media have said if she told them there was no way both her husband and the dealer had died at the same time? There had to be some discrepancy in reports, something to prove the lies.... But no, the murderer had covered his tracks well, except for one small detail.

She knew he was the very man responsible for the murder.

Her husband's partner.

Dan Milano.

She had proof.

He had to know it. She wouldn't expose her husband and family like he thought, though, but that didn't matter. She had just become a wild card in a very deadly game.

And she knew, when the funeral was over, neither she nor her daughter would ever be safe here in Zachary again. Or anywhere else in Louisiana, for that matter. She would have to walk away from this funeral, away from her life, away from everything she knew, or risk exposing Dan...and her husband, for the terrible secret they both had held.

Father God, strengthen me for what I must do.